So right

right

REBEKAH WEATHERSPOON

Books by Rebekah

VAMPIRE SORORITY SISTERS
Better Off Red
Blacker Than Blue
Soul to Keep

STAND ALONES
The Fling
At Her Feet
Treasure

THE FIT TRILOGY
Fit
Tamed
Sated

SUGAR BABY NOVELLAS
So Sweet
So Right
So For Real

Praise for Rebekah's work

"There are actually more really great romance authors out there, but it's only every now and then that you come across writing that makes you say, "This author is going places." Rebekah Weatherspoon is one of those authors." - Pandora Esperanza, *The Last Word Book Reviews*

AT HER FEET

"Indeed, the more I read *At Her Feet* I came to realize that it is the best and most original book that I have read in any genre for a very long time." – Jim Lyon, *The Seattle PI*

FIT

"I felt satisfied by a complete story at the end, and would highly recommend this to anyone looking for a fun, relatable contemporary romance." - Elisa Verna, *Romantic Times Book Reviews (TOP PICK REVIEW)*

TAMED

TREASURE

Dedication

This book is absolutely for the readers,
especially those of you who embraced Kayla
and all her big girl goodness.

Chapter One

I woke up feeling so good. I stretched, pulling the covers back up to my bare shoulders, basking in the warmth of our sheets. If you asked me a year ago if I was happy, I would have said yes. A year ago, I had a job that took care of all my needs, and a cute apartment. I had a roommate who I thought was a great friend, loving parents and twin siblings who thought I was the coolest big sister in the world. The parents still loved me and my sisters still thought I was pretty neat, but I'd lost my job, and then me and my roommate almost ran out of money and decided that the fine life of sugaring was right for us. It absolutely wasn't, but then I met him, Michael Bradbury, for real for real Internet billionaire and now everything was different.

A year ago I didn't know butt from crap about happiness. Now, I had a job I actually wanted. The roommate who turned out to be less than a friend was out of my life. With a little help from said billionaire I was able to rescue my best friend Daniella from her boring corporate job at Telett Wireless and together we had opened Cards by K&D, a greeting card company for the millennial set. Our first official line, Queer Qards by K&D, was due to launch in a few months at L.A. Pride. I had no idea just how awesome it could be to work for yourself and *that* made me pretty damn happy. And then there was Michael.

On the surface, Michael and I made no damn sense. There was the age gap and the bank account gap, and the fact that some dudes don't like girls as thick and juicy as me, and some black girls like me didn't mess with older white guys, but beneath it all we were both just two big nerds who got excited about bad food and things like graphic design and user experience. Before him I had no idea what it felt like to be so in love. I had no idea what it was like to be in a relationship with someone so considerate and so kind. Now when people waxed poetic about soul mates and true partners I knew they weren't lying because I had found that in Michael. He also asked me to move in with him so now I had an even nicer, cuter place to live.

I rolled over to the sound of his fingers moving across his keyboard. Didn't matter if we had a late night or not, didn't matter that it was Saturday either. For Michael, every morning it was early to rise and right to work. The sun was up and I'm sure birds were chirping somewhere; I just couldn't hear them through the double paned windows of his Malibu home. Our home. But the smell of breakfast wafting down the hall made the perfect scene complete.

We had plans for our Saturday morning, adorable couple-y things to do, but it was still too early for Michael to look so good. His long black hair was sporting a few more grays, catching up with his salt and pepper beard and mustache. His thick locks were down, falling around his shoulders, hanging down his back, still all messed up from the great sex we'd had the night before. I knew I was still feeling the effects of our love making turned rowdy fucking. My thighs were a bit sore, and my pussy was still wet. It was a bird chirping kind of day.

"Good morning," I said, my voice a little scratchy from sleep. I couldn't help but smile when he glanced over at me. Those blue eyes.

"Morning, baby. Are you excited?" His lips tipped up a bit at the corner, his version of a smile. He was always so calm and introspective. Only a few people in his life got to see the real thing. Only I got to see him this naked.

"Do you want my honest answer?"

"No. Lie to me. All day long. I hate honesty in a woman."

"I know. Liars are where it's at. Um, yeah. I'm stupid excited."

"Well then. I think we should get going." He leaned over and lightly kissed my cheek before he closed his laptop and slid it down to the foot of our massive bed. I'd just recently started calling it our bed. And our house. I'd been living with Michael in his sprawling modern home in Malibu for almost ten months, but it took me a long time to get over the fact that I wasn't just a visitor. I lived with my boyfriend and it was totally fine for me to make myself comfortable.

And I would have been completely comfortable if Michael's house—our house—wasn't ninety-seven percent glass. The massive windows that made up most of the exterior walls afforded an amazing view of the ocean and the mountains of Malibu, but at night it also felt like a horrifying glass box that was just begging to be burgled. Michael travelled a lot, leaving me alone with his housekeeper, Holger.

I loved Holger's big German ass, but when he was done with his work for the day, his time was his and he spent that time in the pool house. I couldn't ask him to spend the night up in the main house every night Michael was away. He didn't get paid to babysit me. We had a big fence and a gate that could only be opened with a seven-digit code, and Holger could probably hear me screaming if an intruder got by all of that, but there was only one thing that would make me feel completely safe, and Michael agreed.

I reached under the sheets and drew my freshly manicured nails up his toned thigh. "Is Holger still mad?"

"Do you want to go feel him up like this? Butter him up a little?"

"I would if I thought it would work."

"It's that serious, huh?"

"Yes. Baby. We need a puppy."

"You're right," he said with a firm nod. He pursed his lips. "We should get some food in that belly and then hit the road."

I watched Michael as he climbed out of bed, leaving my hand sad and lonely on the warm spot he left in the sheets. I took every inch of him in. The curtains were drawn, but our bedroom was nicely lit by the morning sun. That body. It was sinful for a man at any age. Perfect ass, stacked and toned.

Muscles and tattoos, tanned skin dusted with dark hairs in all the right places. He came around my side of the bed, heavy dick hanging between his legs, probably a little hard from the way I had just been touching his leg. He headed toward the bathroom, and a shower, I guessed, but like he said we still had plenty of time before the shelters opened.

I reached out and caught his fingertips before he could get away. He stopped walking and looked down at me. "Am I being too demanding if I ask you to come back to bed?"

"It depends on what you want me to do if I get back in bed." He moved a little closer and toyed with my fingers.

"Share your penis with me," I said with a pout, watching as his eyes narrowed with just the slightest bit of annoyance.

"Last night, after you came the third time—"

"The fourth. What? I came like five times really, but like four big ones. But do go on. You were saying," I said smiling back with my toothiest grin.

"After you came, I was nowhere near done, but last night when we were coming back from dinner, what did you tell me?"

"I may have said that I wanted to get up early so we could be the first ones to the shelter."

"That's exactly what you said. You can't keep toying with my penis like this," he said, putting his hands on his perfectly sculpted hips. I looked him up and down, starting at those hips and then down lower to the erection that looked like it wanted to come out to play. My eyes wandered up some more to the massive eagle tattoo whose wings covered half his chest and half of his back. And I looked further up, to his perfectly full lips.

"I'm sorry I'm so mean. Here, let me repay you before we go." I gave his hand a solid tug and pulled him back under the covers with me. When he was comfortable I did the only sensible thing and climbed on top of him. It took nothing to slide a little lower so my pussy was rubbing along the length of his quickly hardening dick. My eyes closed as his hands traced the length of my spine. I shifted against him some more, growing wetter every second.

"I'll stop being a dick," I said quietly before I leaned down and kissed his perfect lips. There was a faint hint of sweetened coffee on his breath. I didn't give him shit for being up *and* caffeinated.

"Good," he said when I pulled back just enough. "You know I'll give you whatever you want." I was being a dick still, teasing him, rubbing myself up and down all over him.

"And I'll give you whatever you want."

"Then stop fucking teasing me." That was enough to make me come, how he could go from sweet to filthy in no seconds flat.

"I think I need some assistance."

"You always seem to catch me in my most charitable moods. Let me see what I can do for you."

His hands moved down to my waist, lifting me just enough so my wet slit opened for him. He was big and thick, but every time my pussy took every inch of him.

I sat up just enough to place my hard nipples

right on his mouth, my breath rushing through my teeth as he teased me with his tongue. I couldn't help but ride him hard, couldn't resist fucking myself fast and rough on his thick length.

This was what Saturday mornings were for. Caffeinated kisses and perfect sex.

"Did I mention how excited I am? We're getting a dog, dude," I said as the first hints of an orgasm slid over me. Michael's laughter sputtered around my boob.

"Kayla. Please. Focus." His teeth scraped my tender skin and then he bit down. There was no way Holger didn't hear me coming from the kitchen.

I did want us to be the first people at the West Los Angeles Animal Shelter, but by the time we stopped fucking and by the time I finished repairing the damaged I'd done to my hair by not sleeping in a scarf, I knew we'd probably be the second or third people there. Luckily we'd already picked up a crate and other odds and ends to help our new puppy settle in. Holger was vehemently against bringing animals into the house, but he lost the argument two to one. We were going to get that fucking dog.

I came out into the kitchen and found Michael and Holger glued to the TV. "What's going on?" I asked.

"Good morning, sweet heart." Holger always

separated the words. "Here's your breakfast." He set a plate with a massive omelet and some fruit at the table setting right next to the remains of Michael's breakfast.

Michael glanced away from the TV for a moment, flashing me a warm smile as he held out his hand. I grabbed my plate and came around the other side of his stool so I could stand between his legs while he watched TV. Some player from the Miami Flames was talking about showing up that night for the fans.

"What's the haps?" I asked.

"Steven just texted me and told me to turn it on."

When we met, Michael had been in talks to purchase L.A.'s NBA team from its aging owner, but at the last minute the deal fell through when the owner's son decided he wanted to keep the team in the family. Michael had been disappointed, but he'd shaken it off and moved on to other things, like investing in my business with Daniella. Still, he'd been a lifelong basketball fan, and whenever he was in town we used his courtside season tickets. He always followed the action in the league.

The program cut back to the woman at the broadcast desk. "That was Ladarian Thomas sharing his thoughts on tonight's game against Dallas. Again for those just tuning in, this morning it has been confirmed that Miami Flames owner, Jonathan Taylor Wayne, has been arrested in connection with the contract killing of Orlando resident Arnold Foster over alleged gambling debts. We are expecting a statement from the league commissioner shortly."

"Holy shit," I said under my breath.

"Yeah. That's pretty serious," Michael said as he gave me a little affectionate squeeze on my side.

We continued watching the coverage of the story, as another reporter picked up the report. In addition to being the team's owner, Jonathan Taylor Wayne, who also owned majority stock in Clast Airlines, had apparently been involved in a small but high-stakes gambling ring. I hadn't heard about Arnold Foster's murder, probably because it hadn't made the national news, and after pulling his name up on my phone I found some more details. He'd been shot to death in his car while driving through Orlando three months ago, execution style. Apparently the triggerman had come forward and named the owner of Miami's team as the one who had hired him. It was some movie of the week type shit. When it got to the point where they were rehashing information we already knew, we finished up breakfast and our coffee.

"We'll be back in a couple hours," Michael told Holger as he slipped on his hoodie. Casually dressed Michael was just as hot as all-business Michael.

"Wonderful."

"Cheer up, man. A dog will bring much needed energy to this place."

"I am completely satisfied with the level of energy Kayla has brought to your home." I tried not to laugh in Holger's face. Six foot six and nearly as wide, mohawk and all, and there he was huffing and puffing like an exhausted child.

"Sorry. She wants a dog. She's getting a dog."

Holger glared at me for a moment before a small smile cracked under his handlebar mustache. "Well yes. Resisting the desires of that dimpled face is a fruitless effort."

"We can name it after you if you want," I teased.

"Absolutely not. Just help me clean up after it. I signed on for one man. Now I have a man, a woman, and a mongrel to look after."

"And you are nicely compensated for all of your hard work," Michael reminded him.

"Now is not the time to bring up those types of particulars," Holger huffed as he moved our breakfast dishes over to the sink.

Michael rolled his eyes then took my hand. "We'll be back."

There were a few other people when we arrived at the animal shelter, but I think we had first dibs on the dogs. The family in front of us in line had a very hyper kid, around five or six years old, who was over the moon about picking out a new cat. When it was our turn Michael might have ribbed me a little as I tried to play it cool when the woman behind the counter asked how she could help us.

"Can you show us what you have in a puppy? A large breed perhaps?" Michael said like he was ordering a fine bottle of wine. I rolled my eyes, but laughed with the shelter attendant.

"We do, actually." She pointed us toward the sound of dozens of barking dogs and told us to have a look.

There were so many dogs. I felt terrible, but short of opening our own dog rescue there wasn't much I could do. Michael stopped at the third stall where the cutest grey pit bull puppy was yapping at the fence.

"Penny. Done. Found my dog," Michael said.

"Oh my god, she's so cute."

"She's mine. Keep it moving, sister."

"What? She's great. Let's take her. A pit will murder anything that comes through the door." This was the dog I needed.

"You seemed to want something in the way of a small horse. Keep looking." I looked at him for a second, but he ignored me, squatting down so little Penny could lick his fingers through the fence. "Hey girl," he cooed sweetly.

"Oh. My. God. You want your own puppy. I thought you just wanted one."

"A man is allowed to change his mind."

"A man is full of shit is what he is," I laughed.

Just then one of Michael's phones rang. He straightened instantly and pulled his business cell out of his pocket.

"This is Michael—She's mine. Back off." I glared at him and kept moving down the line. "Richard, hi. Sorry. My girlfriend and I are picking up a dog." I looked back trying to figure out which

Richard he was talking to. He did business with like five. Michael nodded toward the exit then headed outside to take his call.

Like the woman said, there was a mutt puppy that must have been part Newfoundland. It looked more bear cub than dog. It was so cute, but I could just imagine all that fur everywhere. Holger would kill us. There was also some Cujo looking creature that lunged at the fence, barking it's fucking face off as soon as I walked by. I screamed and jumped out of the way like I was at a damn haunted house.

As soon as my brain reminded me of the fence between me and the monster, I moved on to the last stall. My heart still beating in my throat and shoes nearly filled with fear pee, I found another shorthaired puppy, silver with black and white spots and solid black ears and feet. He was a baby, but he had the big clumsy puppy paws that just told you one day you'd be able to throw a saddle on him and rent him out to kiddie parties. The name Patch was on his cage.

He came over to the gate and jumped, trying to lick my hand. He'd make a lousy guard dog, but at least I wouldn't be alone. Michael still wasn't back so I walked back up front.

"I think we're going to take Penny and Patch," I told the woman behind the desk.

"Great!"

Michael came back as they were getting the paperwork ready. I didn't like the frown on his face. "What's going on?"

"Nothing. That was Richard Sands. I might

have to go to New York. We'll talk about it in the car."

"'Kay," I said, letting it go. We didn't need to talk shop at the animal shelter counter, but I grabbed his hand anyway.

Penny was good to go, shots and all, but we had to make an appointment to get Patch fixed in the next few months. And then we had two extremely rambunctious puppies on our hands.

"Holger is gonna kill us," I said after we walked them around the block and got them settled on the blanket we'd put down in the backseat of Michael's G-Class. I climbed back up front and fastened my seatbelt. "So what's going on?"

The frown came back to his face. "They want me to purchase Miami."

"Really? That's great, right? This is what you wanted."

"I wanted to purchase an L.A. team. Miami is a different situation. And the L.A. deal was simple. This is a fucking PR disaster." Michael handled press just fine under pressure, but the kind of press he did was interviews with tech magazines and the occasional rich people publications. He'd never been involved in a legit scandal. Still, I wanted to encourage him to go for it.

One, Michael was actually a good man and with his calm, caring personality and his freakish ability to focus on the right thing, I thought he would be the perfect person to bring the team back together after John Taylor Wayne had his day in court. But this was his call and all I could do was support his choice.

That's how we did things on Team Bradbury-Davis. Mutual support. It felt so good.

He was quiet for a while as we made our way back to the PCH, but suddenly he pulled out his phone. Ruben's name flashed across the dashboard.

"Yes, sir." The voice of Michael's assistant and my good friend chimed through the speakers.

"Hey, sorry to bother you. I have to fly to New York tonight. I need you to come. Am I fucking up your plans?"

"Tonight?" I said a little too loud, my stomach dropping. I instantly wanted to take back my whining, but the puppies!

"Is that my Kay-Kay?"

"Hey Ruben."

"Did you get the puppy?"

"Puppies. Michael cracked and got one for himself."

"Oh yay! Take pictures. I'll come over and play with them when we get back."

"You'll see Penny tonight," Michael added. "Let the crew know we'll be plus one dog."

"What?" Ruben and I said at the same time.

"She's not a Pomeranian, babe. She's a pit bull," I reminded him. Penny was plenty small to carry, but...

"You got a pit bull puppy?" Ruben asked, his shock justified. Pits had a bad rep for sure, but even I didn't have to struggle to imagine just how much more intimidating people would find Michael with a pit bull in his board meetings.

"The sign said she was pit bull/lab mix, but

yeah, and another mutt. PJ and I'll pick you up at seven."

"Great. See you then."

The call ended and Michael wasted no time reaching over and rubbing the back of my neck. "I'm sorry. I have to do this. Richard wants me to meet with the commissioner, just to talk. I think this gambling ring, the conspiracy, everything might be bigger than Wayne."

"Like within the NBA?"

"Yes. They want to get the process of replacing him started immediately."

"Yeah, okay. You should definitely go." I looked back at the puppies, kissing Michael's wrist as I turned my head. Patch was relaxed, looking up at me with his big green eyes, ignoring Penny while she sniffed and batted at his ear. "I'll see if Daniella wants to come over."

"Sounds like a good idea. Are her and Duke still—"

"I don't know." My best friend and Michael's good friend were sort of an item. Problem was, Duke Stone, international pop star and mega producer had a crazier schedule than Michael's. Combine that with Daniella's fear of getting her heart broken and you had the perfect recipe for a will they, won't they. I pulled out my phone and sent her a text.

Busy tonight?

Nope. Watching movies with sister. Duke's on timeout.

You and sister want to come over tonight? You can tell

me what he did and meet my new puppy.

Hell yes. I could use some puppy time.

Michael would be leaving around six so I told them to come around five thirty so they could catch Penny before Michael took her on her first airplane ride. With my evening resolved, I sent Holger a text.
Coming home with two puppies. I'm sorry.

He sent a series of emoticons that made how he felt about our impulse grab perfectly clear.

Chapter Two

We'd had one small tinkle accident but in hour eight of his new life, Patch was doing just fine, snuggled between Daniella and I on one of the bed-like couches in Michael's screening room. Our screening room. A thousand movies to choose from and we'd settled on reruns of *Say Yes To The Dress*. Daniella had shown up with her sister Lili, our social media manager at K&D. I'd tried to get our other friend Gordo to leave the HR department at Telett to come work with us, but he had just gotten promoted and wanted to see the new position through. Lili was young and smart, very social media savvy and sick of working at Popeye's so we gave her the gig. It was a perfect fit.

They arrived just before Michael's driver came to take him to the airport. We played with the dogs, had the delicious dinner Holger prepared for us by the pool, then settled in with our reality TV, and Daniella still hadn't spilled what was going on with Duke.

I looked over as she checked her phone. I'd checked mine too, for the hundredth time, looking at the pictures Michael had sent me of Ruben holding Penny on the jet. I knew they were busy. Ruben might have been Michael's personal assistant, but he was also his sounding board. Ruben was a great listener and gave extremely sensible business advice. And even if Michael just needed to talk his strategy through out loud, Ruben was the one man you wanted in the room to do a little eavesdropping.

I fought the urge to text Michael again and turned to my friend.

"Okay, you gotta dish. What's going on with Duke?" They'd been seeing each other on and off for as long as Michael and I had been an item. They were definitely sleeping together, but for a whole bunch of reasons they couldn't seem to move from fuck buddies to going steady for good.

"He told her he loved her," Lili said.

"Via text," Daniella added. "Via text."

I bit the inside of my lip as Lili rolled her eyes. I had thoughts and feelings, but I didn't want to give them up and make Daniella feel worse.

"I know it's not the same as a handwritten note but maybe—"

"No. I don't care if snapchat love is a way of life for some people. If you're going to tell me you love me, you tell me to my fucking face."

"So, well, wait. What exactly happened?"

"He's in Miami right now working on De'Bonay's new album, which yay holy shit. I can't wait until she goes on tour again, but he wanted me to come with him."

"Is that bad?" I asked carefully.

"No, I just—I don't want to just kick it in the studio. I love what we have going on at K&D. I actually like going to work in the morning now. And now we have an office dog?"

"You want me to bring Patch to the office?"

"Yes," Lili said without hesitation.

"Uh yeah. Of course," Daniella went on. "The perks of owning your own business. You make the rules. But that's not the point. I just wish he were more like Michael. Michael has this wild, exciting life. He's on his private jet as we speak, but he keeps everything so normal for you. Well as normal as things can be with Holger in the house."

A chuckle slipped out as I nodded in agreement but I kept my mouth shut again because any comment I could add, even to refute Daniella's opinion of our relationship was too fucking cheesy for words. With Michael it was effortless. Yes, there was a lot of traveling, and meetings, and weird twenty minute pop-ins at charity events when Michael would have rather just sent a check but, even with the spur of the moment-ness, I got to be with him and I got to see him do things that made him happy. Michael loved to work.

And then, even when he was up to his eyeballs in contracts and app redesigns, and ad approval, he went out of his way to make me happy. I didn't have to work, and I knew it from day one per the terms of our initial Sugar baby/Sugar Daddy arrangement, but when my designs started catching a little traction online I knew I had more than a hobby on my hands. He didn't just sign a check and wish me the best of luck.

Michael was with us every step of the way, helping us find the perfect office space between our house and Daniella's apartment. Suggesting that we needed a social media manager to start, helping us find the right people to build our website and teach us about stuff like mailing lists, and click through and conversion rates. He'd even helped us set up stuff like company health insurance so Daniella could get her HRT and other needs covered. Lili also wanted a vision and dental plan. And even though he was our financial backer, the company was ours, smooth and legal, and Michael had done all that to make me happy.

Was I bummed that he was gone for a few days? Shit yeah, but I knew he'd back soon. We'd kiss and hug, and I'd try to suck his soul out through his penis and after he did his best to dislocate my hip, we'd cuddle with our new puppies and things would be back to normal. I liked Duke a lot, but between recording, performing, and producing for other artists, I had no freaking clue what normal meant to him.

"What do you want to do?"

"I don't know," Daniella said with a miserable sigh. "He sent the text and I was so...bothered by it I called him right back."

"And?"

"And he was drunk. They'd been recording for thirteen hours, but they'd finally nailed the song so they were celebrating."

"Oh."

"Yeah. So I don't even know if he meant it or if he was in some weird drunken sleep deprivation zone. Or feeling lonely because De'b is doing a lot of love songs on this one or what."

"That dress is fucking hideous," Lili blurted out.

Daniella and I both looked up at the mermaid-flared monstrosity. "I'm way too fat for that cut. You'd rock it though."

"I would, wouldn't I?" Daniella said flashing me a big grin.

"You and Michael headed to the altar any time soon?" Lili asked.

"Ho no, I don't know."

"He not the marrying type?"

"Actually I'm not sure he is. I can see him being completely fine just being my boyfriend forever."

"You two should totally get married and have all the babies. You already got dogs, which people say is like baby practice. Why not take it all the way?" Daniella said. She liked Michael for me so much she'd been teasing me about marrying him from the moment we started dating.

I gave Patch's side an affectionate rub, tilting my head as the next bride-to-be stepped up on the riser in a champagne colored ball gown. "I could see myself marrying him though, I guess."

"First step, puppies. Next step, marriage license," Lili teased.

"Yeah," I said with my own laugh. "We'll see about that."

"Anyway I told Duke we'd talk when he was done recording."

"Yes, sorry. Back to you. When will that be?"

"De'bonay's last album took eighteen months and they've been at it for exactly three weeks."

"Dude!"

She shrugged, rolling her phone between her palms. I realized then how glossy her big brown eyes were getting.

I took her hand and pulled her closer, careful not to squish the puppy. "I'm sorry." She let me cuddle her for a few seconds before she pulled away, wiping her face.

"It's so stupid. We have no future together. I mean I like him a lot, but I don't want be with a literal rock star. It's just too much." I didn't know what part of it was too much, maybe all of it, but I saw where she was coming from. Michael was rich, but he wasn't famous. Duke was a star and sometimes you could get burned standing too close to that much light.

My phone vibrated in my hand as a bride tearfully said yes to this dress that did nothing for her cleavage.

It was a text from Ruben, a picture of Michael stretched out with Penny asleep on his chest.

How fucking cute is this shit?

I smiled to myself, my chest hurting a little as I texted back.

Cute as so much fucking shit.

I couldn't wait for Michael to come home.

A few days turned into a week and a half. It was looking like Michael was going to buy the team, but a lot had to be discussed in New York at the NBA headquarters and then they wanted Michael to go to Miami to meet with Rick Chase, the team's GM. Meanwhile, even though he was out on bail, John Taylor Wayne was refusing to give up the team, saying once he'd proved his innocence he'd "be back for another great season." I mean okay, I guess, but allegations of murder for hire were pretty hard to come back from. If the commissioner's office got their way, then Wayne would be forced out and Michael would become the team's new owner.

Holger and I had made a ton of progress in our puppy training with Patch, who had settled in nicely to his role as office pup as well as guard dog. Our mail lady loved him, but while my dog and our large German friend were great company, and work kept Daniella, Lili and I plenty busy, I was starting to go through Michael withdrawal. We talked all the time and texted constantly. And there was phone sex and video chat sex, but boy did I want my man to come home.

He crushed me when he called that following Tuesday night on video chat to give me a status report, telling me he had two more days on the road.

"Can you tell how hard I'm trying not to bitch and moan right now?" I said looking at his slightly pixelated, but still hot as hell face on my laptop screen. I was sitting on the floor beside the bed with my computer on top of our messy sheets. The TV was providing the white noise and companionship a dog couldn't.

"I miss you too, baby," Michael said. "But I'll be back before you know it. You want to go to Half Moon Bay this weekend?"

"Oh is that all? Just a quick jaunt to Half Moon Bay?" I'd been wanting to go to NorCal resort town for months now, but we couldn't find the time.

"Somewhere in the Europe more your speed?"

"No, crazy. Half Moon Bay with you would be perfect. I'd love to go."

"Good. I'll have Ruben call ahead and tell them we're bringing the dogs. I picked the right pooch. Penny travels like a champ." I looked over my laptop screen at my own puppy who was snoozing at the foot of the bed, where he'd been sleeping every night that week, crate be damned.

"Hopefully Patch can handle the plane."

"I'm meeting Duke at the studio for a bit tomorrow and then I have a few more meetings. Then I fly back to New York to meet with Steven so we can talk about shifting some of my responsibilities."

"So you're doing this. You're buying a professional basketball team."

"Yes, I believe I am." Michael glanced down. He was twirling one of his cell phones on the edge of the hotel desk. He was thinking of something. Something that was bothering him. "I need you to tell me if you're not okay with this. There will be a few changes for us. Nothing bad, but different." He looked up at the screen again.

"Of course I'm okay with this. Babe, this is like your dream, even if it's a little different from the original plan. Craziest thing happens, we move to Miami or at least get a place there and I can work remotely with Daniella, but that's not a big deal or a bad thing. I'm excited for you."

Another pause on his end. God, this whole situation must have been hitting him harder than I realized. It was a big deal, a huge decision, but Michael had gone from two bucks away from welfare to one of the richest men in the country. He could do this.

"Babe," I said quietly. "I'm with you."

He sucked in a deep breath and sunk back in his chair. "Thank you."

"Tell Duke I say hi. And Steven." Michael's business partner was the sweetest.

"I will. Stand up. I want to see what you're wearing." Apparently his mood had changed.

"Do you, now?" I said as I stood up anyway, tilting the screen back. I wasn't wearing anything particularly sexy, just a pair of pajama shorts and a cami with one of those faux bras that didn't actually support my huge boobs. Michael was still in his dress shirt and, I assumed, his slacks.

"Get the dildo you like, the clear one."

I quickly reached for the bottom drawer of my nightstand and grabbed my favorite toy, shaped to hit all the right spots. I sat back on my heels, the soft area rug around our bed cushioning my knees. I waved the dildo in the air for him to see.

"Now what?"

"Pull your tits out. I want you to lean over the bed, just the way you were sitting. I want you to fuck yourself."

"You don't want me to get on the bed?" I asked as I pulled the front of my top down, exposing my breasts.

"No, I just want to see your face. I want to watch you come." I moved to pull my shorts and my underwear off, but Michael stopped me. "Nah uh. I see how small those shorts are. Move them to the side."

I smiled, feeling instantly wet. He knew how much I loved his blunt dirty talk. "Are you going to join me?"

He shook his head. "No, I just want to watch."

"Okay. That seems like a horrible idea, but suit yourself." I leaned over just the way he liked, shoving my laptop back on the bed so I'd have more room. I teased myself with the head of the dildo, spreading my slick juices around before I slid the toy inside of my pussy. We'd done this show many times, but it always took me a few minutes to get over the unnecessary, but completely awkward shyness of being watched.

I looked up at the screen, drawn to Michael's intense focus as he looked at me. "I want you home. I want you fucking me."

"Pretend it *is* me. Pretend I'm there with you right now."

I closed my eyes and did just that, bringing up dozens of memories of Michael bending me over the bed. He wasn't a fan of fucking me from behind. He loved looking at my face when he fucked me. He liked to have better access to my nipples. He liked kissing me as we both came, but god he felt so fucking good when he took me that way, his thick cock hitting all the right spots, with the perfect force. And the sounds he made, the quiet subtle groans that slipped out between curse words as I pushed my ass back against his hips.

I moaned, burying my face in the sheets as I came. The orgasm wasn't long, and not nearly enough, but still it took me a minute to get my bearings as I continued to tease my slit with the smooth silicone. I licked my lips, my eyes blinking open as I tried to focus on Michael's face again. Patch made a little huffing puppy noise, but he didn't wake up.

"How was that?" I asked Michael, my chest still heaving. It looked like his hand was moving in his lap, but then it suddenly stilled. He leaned forward.

"It was perfect."

"Come for me," I begged. I wanted to see his dick. I wanted to see his cum all over his fist.

He shook his head, his teeth dragging against the dark hairs just below his bottom lip. "I'm not coming until I get home."

"You're gonna give yourself blue balls. Are you sure that's a good idea?"

"It's the best idea. Trust me. I love you."

"I love you too."

"Get some sleep, baby. I'll talk to you tomorrow." We ended our chat and I climbed into bed, scooting Patch all the way over to Michael's side of the sheets.

The next day I felt like an impatient child. Just one more sleep until Michael was home. I made it through work, spent time running Patch around the yard until he was huffing and tuckered out. Holger retired to his pool house after we ate dinner. I climbed into bed with some design work, but even with the TV on and my puppy by my side I couldn't handle the quiet.

It was late, and it was a school night, but I knew the twins were up. They were never asleep before eleven. Now that they were seniors my parents stopped enforcing a bedtime. I sent Kiara, who never let her phone out of her sight, a text and then hit the video chat icon on my computer. A few seconds later, my baby sister's face popped up on the screen.

"Hey buttface. What are you doing?" I said with a smile.

"Nothing—"

"Hey, Kay!" Kaleigh popped up behind her. They were both dressed for bed with their head scarves on.

"I'm working on my calc homework," Kiara said.

"No she's not. She's on Tumblr talking to

Tommy Jackson."

"Kaleigh, you're such a snitch. Who's Tommy Jackson?" I asked.

"No one. He's in my calc class. That's why I'm talking to him."

"Whatever. He asked me to the Spring Fling last week, because he thought I was her." The twins were identical, but they were so different. Both loud and mouthy, but Kiara was the sensitive one and Kaleigh was our brave one. She'd walk through a maze of spiders just to prove she could. Kiara would sob, but take out her phone and search the Internet for directions around the perimeter.

"Are you going with him?" I asked Kiara.

"Yeah, he finally asked the right twin, but it's not a big deal. We're just going as friends." Kaleigh stood behind her, shaking her head and then she made an obscene gesture.

I just laughed. "Well have fun. Kaleigh, are you going?" She had already lost interest in the conversation.

"Yup, all the track and field girls are going together as a group."

"That should be fun." Just then Patch woke up and made his way up the bed on his awkward, clumsy paws. I leaned away as he tried to lick my face. I'd already sent the girls a hundred pictures of him, but Kiara still cooed at the screen. Kaleigh was looking at her own phone.

"He's so cute," Kiara whined. "I want a puppy."

"When Michael gets back you can video chat

with his dog and then when school is over you can come out to visit and you can play with both of them. Michael's puppy is just as cute."

"We know," Kaleigh said absently, still looking at her phone. "Penny. We met her yesterday."

Kiara's head whipped around. "Leigh!"

My stomach dropped like a bag of dirt at the warning in Kiara's voice. "What do you mean you saw Penny yesterday?" I asked. "We didn't talk yesterday."

My sisters didn't answer right away. Then suddenly the camera on Kiara's phone was facing their ceiling.

"Eh! Yo, I'm still here. Hello!"

I heard them murmur arguing for a few seconds, then Kiara picked up the phone again. She was still looking at Kaleigh.

"What the hell is going on?"

"Um…"

"Just tell her," Kaleigh said. "It'll be worse if she asks him about it."

"Asks him about what? Tell me."

Kiara swallowed, her eyes darting everywhere but in my direction. She took a deep breath. "Okay, but you have to pretend to be surprised. You have to. He'll kill us."

"No he won't," Kaleigh said.

"He won't," I assured them. "Just tell me."

Kiara hesitated a little too long. Kaleigh grabbed the phone out of her hand. "Michael was here yesterday talking to Momma and Daddy."

"About what?"

"Duh, what do you think?"

"Hell, I don't know."

"Oh my god, Kay. You're dumb. Why else would he come all the way here to talk to your parents? To talk to Dad? He was getting their blessing."

"What?"

"He's gonna propose to you."

"What?! When? He really came to the house?" Michael and I had been back to North Carolina to spend Thanksgiving with my family. My whole huge, crazy southern family. He survived the weekend and won most of my family over. One of my aunts was still a little put off by me dating such an older white guy and my mom was just filled with her general mom worry, but everyone else was on board. Michael and my dad got along great. But that was only part of the point.

"Wait. Back up. You know for a fact that Michael is going to propose to me?"

"Yes. He talked to Mom and Daddy while we played with Penny and then he told us that he was going to ask you and asked us if we were cool with it. I mean we're not twelve so that was a little weird—"

"I thought it was sweet," Kiara said.

"Okay, it was cute. But yeah. He's gonna ask, but you can't say anything. You have to be surprised."

From the way, my heart was beating in my neck, I somehow knew that surprised wasn't going to be a problem.

Chapter Three

There's something about being woken up in the middle of the night. Not by a noise or a sudden urge to pee. I'm talking about those nights where you're knocked out, the guest of honor at the sandman's garden party, and suddenly you're being yanked out of all the fun.

I *was* dreaming about being at a garden party with Daniella and someone who was Lili but didn't look like her. We were holding tennis rackets, but there was no court and then I felt something tugging me, and then the dream started to swirl away. I wanted to hold on to it because my body loves sleep and the party really was nice, but I didn't really have a choice.

Still it took me a while to realize exactly what was happening. Someone was kissing my neck. It was Michael, I knew it was Michael, but part of my brain was still in that lush, sun kissed backyard, filled with party guests and little cakes. I couldn't reconcile that with the darkness of the bedroom and the arms sliding around my waist.

I shook, my body finally snapping back to reality and then I let out the most pitiful sob. I wasn't crying, but my chest and my throat flooded with so much emotion I figured the tears would come next.

I rolled into Michael's arm. I tried to speak but

I was still half asleep. "You're back" came out more sounding like "Yurb blath."

Michael's laugh vibrated down to my stomach. "I couldn't wait any longer. I had to see you."

I gave up trying to open my eyes and just smiled as he plied kisses to my cheeks and neck, traveling a familiar path. There was a moment, not so much a spoken question, but I knew he was asking if he could make love to me. I nodded in my sleepy haze, wiggling to help him get me out of my shorts. Then his head was between my legs.

I rocked against him, my eyes still closed, but my body slowly getting with the program. I could feel how much he wanted me. How he couldn't wait until the morning. I was just so happy he was there. I missed his hands, his large hands with their long strong fingers gripping my breast and caressing my thighs. I missed the way my skin reacted to gentle scrapes of his beard and mustache. I came as he sucked my clit into his mouth. A tiny, but perfect explosion that left me soaking wet but sleepier and somehow still craving more.

He climbed up my body then, pushing his way inside me with one slow thrust. He moaned my name. We were both glad he was home.

The next morning I had to deal with the fact that some secrets are the fucking worst, especially good secrets, because you want to tell someone. I wanted to tell Michael that I knew, but even if it wasn't exactly a secret to him, I knew the maximum levels of unchill I would have to reach to tell Michael I knew he was going to propose to me. Didn't stop me from being as giddy as shit as soon as I jumped out of bed, and Michael's behavior didn't help the situation either. I showered and got ready for work. Michael and Holger were in the kitchen with the dogs, watching ESPN.

"This is the most SportsCenter I've ever watched in my whole life," I teased. I thanked Holger for my breakfast and took a seat next to Michael. The reporter was talking more about the situation in Miami, confirming that Wayne was expected to be removed as owner in the upcoming week.

"This is so crazy," I said, but then I realized Michael wasn't looking at the TV anymore. He was looking at me. I smiled back at him, trying not to blurt out YES! to a question he hadn't even asked yet. I settled on "Good morning," and then I leaned forward and kissed him. He reached up and stroked my hair.

"Holger, can you give us a few minutes?"

"Absolutely. Come dogs!" He clapped loudly and Patch immediately fell into step behind him. A confused Penny toddled after.

"I missed you," I said when we were finally alone. "I'm glad you came back early."

"I needed a break from the madness. I think the deal is going to be announced by the end of next week. There's something I wanted to discuss with you."

I tried to hide my smile, but kinda failed in the most spectacular way. "Sure, what's on your mind?" *Cause I'm gonna say fuck yes.*

"I'm going to have interviews and press conferences and still there's about a month left in the regular season, but that covers a lot of games. And then I'll have to prepare for the draft. I'll be back and forth to Miami a lot. I'd like you to come with me."

"Oh, ah, sure."

"I know Daniella's been meeting with local vendors, but she's welcome to join us and of course Lili can come. She can tweet and post on Facebook from anywhere. Ruben's getting us a house squared away for the next few weeks and we can set up an office for you there. When the season's over we can spend some time looking for a place to buy."

"Daniella and Duke are beefing right now, so I don't know if she'll want to risk seeing him."

"He said she was ignoring his calls and texts. I don't want to drag you out of town if you'd prefer to stay here."

"No, no. Hey, I'm coming. This is a pretty wacky adventure. I wouldn't miss it for anything. I'm in."

"Okay," he said, but there was more and I didn't think it had anything to do with the proposal. Something was bothering him. I toyed with the zipper on his hoodie, exposing more of his perfect chest.

"You look like you were worried that I was going to say no and then slap you or something."

"In so many words, that's how I'm feeling right now. This is my dream. I didn't consult you about it first." My heart sunk. Why would he ever...

"My boyfriend owns the Miami Flames. Try to come up with something I'd hate about this."

"A lot of air travel."

"In your private jet or, at the very least, first class if I'm going alone. Try again."

"It's humid."

"Is that all? Anything else you want to talk to me about?"

"No. I've expressed my concern for your overall happiness and well-being."

"Goodbye, Michael," I said with a laugh as I stood up. "I'm going to work." I didn't make it very far before Michael pulled me back and kissed me soundly on the mouth.

"We're still on for Half Moon Bay this weekend."

"I wouldn't miss it."

He kissed me again and gave my ass a light squeeze. "I love you."

"I love you too."

As soon as I got to work I told Daniella and Lili about all the recent developments. They'd both already signed an NDA the moment it was clear that they would be in Michael's life nearly as much as mine, but

I knew I didn't have to worry about them saying anything to anyone about Michael's official purchase of the team. Daniella was a steel trap and Lili was the sort of aloof type who didn't care deeply enough about things to tell other people about them. Of course I couldn't keep my own mouth shut about that other thing.

I plopped down on our office couch with Patch in my lap. I dodged his licks, watching Daniella and Lili's eyes pop wide as I told them about how my sisters spilled the beans.

"Oh my god. Kayla. You're getting married!" Daniella screeched.

"Well not yet, but yeah." Then I might have let out a high-pitched squeal.

"I guess he is the marrying type after-all," Lili said.

"Shit, I guess so."

"You think he'll pop the question this weekend?" Daniella asked. "I mean a spur of the moment trip to Half Moon Bay seems like the perfect time to do it."

"You're right. I don't know. I hope so! I still can't believe he flew to North Carolina to ask my parents. And my sisters. It's so old school, but I know that's what my mom and dad would have wanted. Jesus, I haven't even met his parents yet."

I'd met his brother and sister. Matthew was awesome, and Myra and I had gotten close enough that she just contacted me when she needed to bug Michael about something, but I hadn't met the parents yet. They were back in Michigan. Not that

Michael couldn't afford for us to take a little trip there, but his mother was dealing with dementia and though he didn't talk about it much, Michael wasn't handling it well. I knew he'd introduce me to his folks when he was ready, hopefully before we got married.

"I think he has permission to marry you. He's old enough to do it without his parents' say so," Daniella said with a wink.

"Shut up," I laughed. "Do you guys want to come to Miami?"

"Yes!"

"Ehhhh…" Lili and Daniella said at the same time.

"I want to go, but I don't want to see Duke, and if you and Michael have a spot, I know he's going to come over."

"I would love to go to Miami," Lili said from her desk.

"And there's no way in hell my mom is gonna let her traipse around South Beach."

"What the fuck? I'm twenty-one."

Daniella said something to her in Spanish and then turned back to me. "I know exactly what my mom will say. She knows how charming Cuban men are. She won't be able to resist."

"Oh whatever. Like there aren't plenty of guys for me to get in trouble with right here."

"Exactly, and Mami is responsible for you and whatever trouble you want to get into. We go to Miami and I'm responsible. I don't want that burden on my shoulders," Daniella teased. Then she turned back to me. "When you and Michael get things settled we'll come for a few days."

"That's a great idea. It'll give me a second to figure out what's what while Michael is doing his thing. And in the meantime, we'll get to do fun long distance stuff like have conference calls."

"Yay! Look at us. We are so grown up and professional right now."

"Yeah we are. Which reminds me—"

"You have a shit ton of work to do?" Daniella said.

"Yeah."

I set Patch down on his official K&D mascot doggy bed with something bright and rubber to destroy, then walked over to my desk and plugged my laptop into my monitors. If I was going to be traveling with Michael, I had to spend every available moment getting our new line of cards ready in time for Pride.

With Daniella and Lili's input and several Patch related breaks, I completed three more designs before we called it a day. Michael would completely understand if I had some work to do on our trip but there was no way I was gonna screw up the perfect will-you-marry-me moment because I had my head firmly pointed at my laptop. This weekend would be all about me and him.

I headed home to pack and drop off my car,

and after traffic died down, PJ took Michael, the puppies and me to the airport. Holger offered to look after them for us while we were away, his slick way of saying he didn't actually hate us for getting two dogs and that he was actually growing fond of them, but Michael insisted they come. Patch needed plane training.

And how. After we got Patch to sit the fuck down—he was not a good flyer—the cabin crew served us dinner. Ruben wasn't with us but I was surprised that Michael wasn't on his phone replying to emails. I curled up beside him on the cushy couch that ran up the right side of the cabin and grabbed the remote to the flat screen.

"TV or movie?" I asked as I brought up the guide.

"It's my lady's pick."

"Hmmm, do I really want to watch something or do I just need a little background noise?"

"Background noise for what?"

"For this." I reached over my shoulder and grabbed the beige monogrammed throw that was draped on the back of the couch. I slipped it over Michael's lap, just in case Sandy, the flight attendant, came back to check on us. Then I turned on some movie that looked like Taken 4 or 5. I took my sweet time unbuckling Michael's belt and undoing his fly, looking at the TV the whole time. Ignoring the way he was looking at me and what my hands were doing. He was fully hard when I stuck my hand in his boxer briefs. I snuggled closer, resting my head against his shoulder and slowly started jerking him off.

It took a few cross-country trips, but I was over my insecurities about fooling around with Michael when only a thin door separated us from the crew.

I knew he was enjoying it when he let out a rough puff of air through his nose, but I asked him anyway. "Does that feel good?"

"You know it does."

"You're not going to let me finish, are you?"

"Not a chance, but we can pretend for a few minutes."

I laughed and gave him the gentlest of squeezes before I kept on with my thorough stroking. I think I'd managed to give Michael maybe four hand jobs to completion. It had become a little joke of ours, but every time I tried to jerk him off or give him head he almost never let me finish. He always pounced on me.

"How come you never let me make you come?" I asked him, even though I already knew the answer. "I just want to make you nut all over my chin."

"You know why."

I sat up and looked him in the eye, but I didn't stop. His cock felt so good in my hand. "Tell me again."

"You want me to be dirty about it."

"Yeah." I flashed him a filthy smile.

"I like how good you feel."

"You just like it?"

"I love it." He groaned, stretching and opening his legs a little wider. "Shall I compare it to a summer's day?"

"How good it feels to come in my pussy?" I

said with an uncontrollable snort. "Yes please."

But Michael just shook his head, then pulled me closer and kissed me. I kept stroking him, working him up and down. I was shocked when he told me he was close. He usually tackled me to the floor or the nearest cushy surface before we got to that point. I moved the blanket out of the way so I could watch him spill all over my hand, but at the last second I changed my mind and took him in my mouth. He growled out one of the sexier "Fuck"'s I'd ever heard and then he came in my mouth. I swallowed every drop. He grabbed my hair, holding it back for me as I continued to suck and clean him off.

I sat up and let out a deep breath. "Okay. Now you do me."

Again he was quiet as he smiled at me, but even though his eyes were still a bit bleary, he guided me to my feet between his legs. I watched as he unzipped my jeans and almost came instantly as he shoved his hand into my underwear. Grabbing his wrist and pushing his palm harder against my wet clit seemed like the right thing to do.

"You got what you wanted, my nut in your mouth. So you have to give me what I want."

"That's gonna be the next card I give you," I said on a moan, my hips rocking forward. "A sonnet about your dick and nuts."

"Pure fucking romance. I love it."

I leaned over, bracing myself on Michael's shoulders as he continued to fuck me with his hand. When I came, muffling my cries on his lips, from the way he held on to me, I think I gave him exactly what he wanted.

It was the middle of the night by the time we reached our beachside rental house. Michael suggested I get ready for bed while he took the dogs for some fresh air. I told him that sounded like the start of an episode of Dateline and insisted on going with him. Truth was, even though I was exhausted, I didn't want to be away from him. After we got the dogs situated we both climbed into bed, exchanging light touches and lazy caresses until we passed out. I may have fallen asleep with a smile on my face. There was a very distinct possibility that I would be heading back to the Los Angeles a newly engaged woman.

I did not head back to the Los Angeles a newly engaged woman.

We had a great time. Good food, perfect weather, a-fucking-mazing sex. Sex in the giant bed right in front of the massive French doors that opened to the water. Sex in the spacious kitchen. Sex on the beach right after sunset. We did it that time on top of a sheet. I don't do sand in the crack. Michael even surprised me and fucked me from behind in the shower. All the perfect kissing and cuddling I could handle, nice quiet walks with the puppies. I found out that Michael sucked at checkers and then I found out he just liked letting me win at checkers. The whole time he didn't take any calls. He attended to some emails, and he blew up Ruben's phones with texts because he did have a lot of shit to do once when we got back, but he was all there, attention on me.

There were several different times I thought he might pop the question, over breakfast, on the beach, when I was playing tug of war with Penny and I caught him staring at me with this dreamy look in his eye, but the next thing I knew we were back in the jet, flying somewhere over the long expanse of California and Michael was mid-Monday morning conference call and still, nada. I tried not to be upset. I knew it was stupid to be upset. Well I wasn't really upset, more like disappointed. Knowing you're about to get something so huge, something you didn't think was even on the table and then to have to wait? It was the best tease ever. Still, I knew Michael and I knew he liked to do things his own way. If he was going to ask, he was going to ask at the right time for him.

I shot Daniella a quick text—*On own way back. I'll be in the office tomorrow. I'm available now though. Working on the plane*—then I set to work on more designs and I was making some pretty good progress when Daniella texted me back.

Well?!?!

He didn't ask.

What? Bummer! He will soon.

I hope so. I'm going crazy. I want to kill my sisters for telling me.

True. Kinda ruins the surprise.

And turns me into a crazy person.

HAHA. Patience darling. You'll be Mrs. Michael Bradbury before you know it.

Okay. My impatience sounds creepy when you put it that way.

I glanced up from my phone and found Michael looking at me from across the cabin. He was talking to Steven and a few of their associates about an app for their dating site dedicated to seniors. He threw me a wink that made my chest ache. I gave myself a little internal slap. He was gonna ask when he asked and even if he never popped the question, this was the man I wanted to be with and right there, in that moment, was where I wanted to be. Damn straight. I pulled up his textbox on my phone and sent him a message. Not exactly a sonnet, but...

My cunt is still sore
To whom do I owe this bliss
Your dick n nuts. Sweet.

I hit send and then focused back on my design work, doing my best to ignore the way Michael tried to cough to cover his laughter.

Chapter Four

The next day it was back to the office. More design work for me. So far I had come up with five designs to support people coming out at any age, five gender neutral valentines, two "it's okay if you're still figuring yourself out" type cards and five humorous gender neutral "I love you so much I think about doing things we both find intimate like fisting or going to the zoo" type cards. I wanted to get more specific and fun with my same sex stick figure cards, but I was still happy with my progress.

Daniella and I finally decided on the printer we wanted to use after so, so many test samples, and Lili had gotten into a hilariously adorable online back and forth with whoever was running the Twitter account for Notable Moments, one of the larger greeting card companies. That snagged us another one hundred followers before quitting time. All in, it was a good and busy day, and after I made my way past an accident on the PCH, I was happy to be home. I had crap TV to watch and my man to make sex with.

Patch and I walked in to find Holger finishing up dinner prep. "Hello, my dear. And Patch."

"Hello," I said as I stepped out of my shoes. "That smells delicious."

"Pecan crusted chicken."

"Is my boo thang home? Or does PJ have him

out and about? I saw his car in the garage." Just as I said the words I heard the approaching jingle of Penny's tags. Patch ran to meet her, their clumsy play tangling around Michael's legs as he walked into the kitchen. He'd worked from home all day, but he'd ditched his usual hoodie plus boxers, no shirt, ensemble for jeans, a dress shirt and a blazer. His long hair was up in a ponytail.

I shed my own light jacket and kissed him. "Hello," I said with a smile.

"Good evening. Would you care to join me by the pool for dinner?"

"Absolutely." I giggled as Michael held out his arm. He was more of a hand holder, but still I took hold of his muscular bicep and followed him out to the pool deck. It always looked gorgeous this time of day. The sunset over the rises and valleys of the Malibu terrain just beyond his property, glittering off the ocean that was barely a mile away but seemed to go on forever. The coyotes were out, yipping and calling, egging each other on. The perfect backdrop for the candlelit table right in the middle of the shrouded cabana.

Holger served dinner and dessert as I told Michael about my day. His upcoming business plans were about forty times more interesting, but he listened intently as I talked about the things I was still learning in Illustrator and the fascinating world of card stock.

"You don't know stress until you've been through every version of glossy and matte that six different vendors have to offer."

The corner of Michael's mouth turned up in his signature smile. "You have amazing taste. I can't wait to see the final products."

"Hopefully I'll have something soon." I stretched, pointing my fingers at my toes, and fought the urge to pat my full belly. "What a lovely way to spend a Tuesday night. Thank you."

Then Michael got serious. "There is something I need to speak with you about."

"Okay."

"I'll be right back." He stood abruptly and walked back into the house.

"Oh my god," I breathed the second he was out of earshot. This was really happening. He was really going to do this. I rocked on the bench cushion, trying to keep the restless tapping of my feet under control. Be cool, Kayla. Be cool. Michael's just going to propose. No big deal. Happens all the time.

Michael came back a few minutes later holding his new tablet, this massive beast with a screen bigger than my laptop monitor. He put it down on the table between us and then took a seat, scooting a little closer.

"What's this?" I asked lightly as I read the header at the top of the wall of text. It took a second for my mind to process what the words said. Michael reached up and tucked my hair behind my ear. I usually lived for his gentle touches, but I was fighting the urge to throw up the amazing dinner Holger had just prepared for us. The words *Prenuptial Agreement* punched me in the gut.

"I've been told there is no easy way to bring

this up."

"Something you guys talk about at your billionaire boys' club meetings?" I said, trying to laugh. Michael did let out a little chuckle.

"Yes, something like that. Usually you pop the question first and this comes up some time before the actual signing of the marriage license."

"But?"

"But I don't feel comfortable asking you to make such a major life decision without knowing all the factors."

"Is this—is—are you asking me to marry you?"

"I am. I want you to be my wife and I want to be your husband, but I want you to know that you're taken care of, and if we have children I want you to know that they're taken care of too."

My eyes snapped to his. "Do you *want* to have kids?"

"I do. I know I'm getting up there—"

"No, that's not what I meant. I just—you just—you seem so bachelor-y. The dogs seemed like such a big step for you, a big step for *us*."

"They are. Having *you* here has been a big step for me too. I lived by myself for over twenty years. If you don't account Holger."

"Yeah," I breathed. Or at least I tried. My face was so hot and my head was swimming. "Kids. Yeah, yes. I do want to have kids. Not like right this second, but soonish I guess."

"This is why I wanted to talk to you like this. I love you, but there's a lot we haven't discussed yet. Coming to Miami with me is one thing, but I want us to be on the same page about a real future together. You sound so surprised to hear that I want to have children, I regret not telling you sooner."

"No, no. It's just a lot. Go on."

"Take some time. Read it over." He said something after that, but I couldn't really hear him. The roaring in my ears was too loud. The screen of the tablet was becoming blurry right before my eyes.

Michael placed something else on the table. "—she came highly recommended by Cassandra." I picked up the business card. *Sarah McNamara. Attorney. Beverly Hills.* Cassandra, right. Steven's wife. She was married to a billionaire. She would know what to do. "She can walk you through each section. I don't think you're a murderer, but I had my will amended to include you and your family as well. Kayla."

"Yeah." My voice didn't sound like my own. I turned the card over in my hand.

"I understand if this something you don't want to do."

"What?" I looked up into his bright blue eyes.

"I get it. I'm old as shit and this isn't exactly romantic. It wouldn't be shocking if you had other plans for the rest of your life that didn't involve me. I'll understand—"

"No! No. I'm sorry." My non-reaction was giving him the wrong impression. That's when the tears started rolling down my cheeks. I'm talking huge, fat tears taking turns on the Slip N Slide that was my face. Michael reached up and started wiping them away.

"You can say no and we can just be together."
I knew what he was saying. Michael was so afraid of making me do things I didn't want to do. He knew what his money did to other people, what money did to most people, how it could intimidate and coerce, but it had never been like that between Michael and me. Yeah he was into K&D for a hefty chunk and we lived together. I owed him so much, but Michael had never made me feel indebted to him in that way. We'd never even detoured down that awkward road. I loved him and I never felt for one second like there was anywhere I wanted to be more than with him. I didn't think he would suddenly pull the rug out from under me. I just wasn't expecting *this*.

Clearing my throat, I got with the program. "I—I want to marry you. I love you. Yes. Yes. I'm saying yes."

Michael didn't say anything, but this million watt smile spread across his face, making his gorgeous eyes crinkle in the corners. And then he kissed me. I was having an out of body experience for sure, but I kissed him back, I know that much. I could taste the salt from my tears on both our lips.

He pulled away then, reached into his pocket and pulled out a ring box. When he opened it, I almost choked. The biggest fucking diamond I'd ever seen in real life was floating in a hexagonal diamond halo setting.

"What's that? A CZ?" I laughed through my tears.

"Not even. Shiny plastic and plated copper. It'll probably give you a skin infection." Michael reached for my hand and slid it on my finger. It fit.

I let out a choking sound as Michael took both my hands in his. We were both shaking. "Oh my god," I said, my voice thready and not in a good way. What the fuck was wrong with me?

"Are you okay?" he asked. Even he could tell it was more than just nerves that had me all off kilter.

"Yeah. I think I stopped breathing there for a second." My laughter felt genuine this time, but it still sounded a little crazy. "I love you." I couldn't stop crying.

"The twins helped me pick it out. Kiara said, quote 'This is Kayla. Like so Kayla.'" Michael turned my palm in his so we could look at the ring together. His ring. My ring. He had actually asked me to marry him. I still couldn't breathe, I definitely couldn't think. So my body took control and launched me out of my seat right into Michael's arms.

"Good morning," Daniella said, looking up from her computer screen.

Lili offered her usual, "'Sup."

I grunted something like "Yeah, great," as I dragged my feet over to Daniella's desk.

"Oh no. What's wrong?" I held out Sarah McNamara's business card.

"What's this? Oh my god!" Daniella forgot all about the card and grabbed my hand, turning this way and that so she could peep the ring. "He proposed! Girl, look at that fucking rock."

"I know."

Lili made her way over and gave my shoulder one of those rub pats. "Congrats. What's with the weepy eyes and the business card though?"

"Do we need an attorney for something?" Daniella asked.

"No, I do. To go over the prenup Michael laid on me last night."

"Oh, Jesus."

"Damn." Both of their reactions were fitting.

"That's how he proposed. With the prenup."

"Waywhat?" The way Daniella shook her head was almost cartoonish.

"Super romantic dinner, out by the pool, sunset, delicious food, great dessert and then he proposed to me with a prenup on a tablet." The words came sputtering out and suddenly I was kind of chuckling, but mostly crying hysterically.

"Oh no," Daniella laughed. "Don't cry. Come here." She tugged me over to the couch where I flopped down under the weight of becoming completely unhinged. Lili flopped down on my other side, trying to provide the other piece to their sister sandwich of comfort.

"I've been like this since last night. We, ya know, totally fucked afterward and I was crying while we were having sex," I said, still blubbering.

"But he proposed, right? Isn't that what you wanted?" Daniella asked.

"Yes, but not like this. Not like this!" I shook

my fists dramatically at the ceiling. "Maybe Michael and Duke went to the same charm school."

"Oh my god. I wouldn't doubt it. He will not stop texting me. Like bro, do better."

"I have to call Sarah Whatsherface to confirm, but I'm meeting this attorney today so we can go over the prenup. See if there are any changes I want to make before I sign. That's why I didn't bring Patch today. I don't know how long I'll be over there."

"Okay this isn't ideal or romantic, but Michael is worth like a jagillion dollars. A prenup kinda makes sense."

"I know, but after the ring. After the ring."

"I'm sorry babe."

"It is a great ring though." Lili grabbed my hand so she could get a good look at the diamond. Then Daniella was practically leaning over my lap so she could look at it too.

"I might actually forgive Duke for something like this."

"God, I'm awful. What is wrong with me?"

"Nothing. You want what most women want—shit, most people. Appropriately timed romantic gestures. Not a legal presentation on a tablet. Or a drunken I love you text."

I wiped my face, glad I'd had the foresight to go with waterproof mascara. Daniella was right about everything. The prenup made sense and I was freaking engaged! Still something felt off, other than the fact that I couldn't stop crying tears of confusion. Too bad I couldn't pinpoint what that something was.

The offices of Lawn & McNamara were on the fifth floor of this shiny glass building in Beverly Hills. I left with plenty of time to beat traffic and make my one p.m. appointment, but I got there a little too early, leaving myself with twenty minutes to sit in the waiting room and just stew over what had happened in the last twenty-four hours. I couldn't stop looking at my ring. It was part amazement, part shock and a lot of just getting used to lugging the thing around.

It was beautiful though, I thought as I pushed the band to right a little, then back to the left. That's when Sarah McNamara came out to the lobby and found me, looking sad for no fucking reason, toying with my giant engagement ring.

Sarah was not at all what I was expecting. Actually I had no clue what I was expecting, but I was shocked when a short and round Asian woman closer to my age introduced herself and led me back to a conference room. She was pleasantly chubby like me, but her high-waisted skirt and matching blazer were perfectly tailored, her long hair freshly trimmed with the sharpest bangs going straight across her forehead and she was wearing an assortment of Tiffany's finest, yet subtlest pieces. She was sporting her own wedding band and sizeable diamond ring to match. "I'm so glad you could make it," she said with a bright smile.

"Thank you for helping me. I get the basic legal

stuff, but this sort of thing is not my area of expertise."

"That's what I'm here for." She held the conference room door for me and ushered me inside.

Everything was set up all nice and professional. The prenup was there, right on the table with along with pens, a highlighter and some sticky notes. There were some water glasses and a little arrangement of fruit, like refreshments would be necessary to get through this torture.

Sarah caught me staring at the spread.

"Sometimes these things take a while. Also talking money and divorce before you even pick out your wedding dress tends to make people a little anxious, so having something to nibble on can help with the anxiety."

"Good call."

"Go ahead and have a seat."

I took the chair closest to the window and set my bag down. I tried to look anywhere but at the table. That worked for three whole seconds. The document seemed so much longer and thicker when it was printed out. I looked at the papers. My whole future with Michael in black and white, on crisp 8x11 sheets that had probably just lost the heat from the printer the moment I walked in the door.

"Did you get a chance to look this over?" Sarah asked as she took the seat beside me.

"Uh, no I didn't. He—um he just asked last night and then we celebrated. And then I had to go into work this morning."

"I completely understand. It's tempting to just

sign and not even bother with the fine print, but we want to make sure that you understand everything proposed here and that you're comfortable with it."

I shifted in my seat and adjusted my skirt. I might as well have grabbed the collar of my shirt to let out the excess steam.

"It's okay to be nervous," Sarah said. "You find out a lot about a person when it comes to their terms, but I can tell you now that Mr. Bradbury definitely has your best interests in mind. Let's get started."

"Okay." I leaned forward and forced myself to focus.

The plan was to go through the whole document once. Then we'd go through it again if I had questions or things I wanted to change. If I was okay with everything, we'd use the final pass for me to add my initials and signatures.

Michael (or his attorney) had thought of everything. In the event of our divorce, due to irreconcilable differences, I'd get a certain lump sum and more paid out in monthly installments. If we had kids, that amount increased. If we broke up because of infidelity on my part, I still got a shit ton of money. If he cheated, I got even more. The house in Malibu would be his no matter what, but if we split up he'd buy me a home of equal value. I needed a break at that point.

Sarah understood.

After I chugged some water and shoved two strawberries in my mouth we kept going. Even though it hadn't been announced yet, the Miami deal was done. Michael, of course, got the team. He got

Penny and I got Patch. I prayed that our marriage outlasted the dogs.

"I know including the pets seems a little strange," Sarah said. "But people become really attached to their animals. Custody battles over dogs or cats or even birds can get just as ugly as custody battles over kids."

"Yeah, it makes sense," I managed to say. I didn't sound like myself.

We went on. I got to keep everything Michael ever bought me. What the fuck would he want with purses and shoes and plus-size lady panties, I wondered, but then Sarah reminded me again, my silence prompting her, that divorce sometimes made people ridiculous and petty.

"Some people want to leave their ex-spouse with literally nothing." I pictured Michael doing just that, leaving me with nothing but the ripped jeans and toothbrush I arrived at his house with. He would never do something like that. It wasn't in his nature, but thanks to this stupid document I was thinking about it.

"Are you okay Miss Davis?" I looked up at Sarah the moment I realized I was staring blankly at the center of the table.

"Yeah, it's just a lot."

"Listen, this is my job, this is what I do and I can tell you have a good man here. Whatever happens, he doesn't just want you taken care of. He wants you happy and comfortable. That's a good thing."

"Yeah. Thanks."

I had questions, but no changes. Sarah explained every last detail and though I know I should have felt relieved when I initialed here and there and signed at the bottom there, and don't forget the date there, once it was all said and done, I still couldn't shake the strange feeling. I grabbed my bag and followed Sarah back out to the lobby where she shook my hand.

"We'll get this over to his people. Beyond that I'm fairly certain we'll never have to see each other again."

"Jesus Christ, I hope not."

I had plenty of time to get back to my office, but I went to Michael's office instead. I'd only been there once before. Michael had given me security clearance to get past the front desk in the downstairs lobby, but the new receptionist in the ICO offices looked at me like I was fucking insane when I asked to see Michael. And no, I didn't have an appointment and yes, I am his girlfriend, a reaction I was used to from skinnier white women who thought they were cuter than me.

I wasn't going to tell her I was his fiancée since I didn't know if there was some sort of internal press release protocol at ICO when it came to Mr. Bradbury's personal life. But I know she saw the ring when I checked my phone. Her eyes almost popped out of her head.

Ruben came and got me. He joked with the girl, Kiersten or something, about her boyfriend, which distracted her from my presence for a second but I didn't miss the look of shock and awe that returned to her face as we turned away.

"Lemme see the new bling," Ruben said instead of hello. "Oh this is way better than the ring I picked out."

"How many people weighed in on this thing?"

"Just me and Myra and Holger. But your sisters set him straight. Fuck, girl, that's beautiful."

"Thanks. It's heavy."

"Cause it's real," he said with a wink.

He led me back through the ultra modern office space where the employees at ICO were hard at work. Phones ringing, keyboards clacking. A burst of laughter from a far corner that was immediately silenced with a snort. Regular office life. I didn't miss it at all.

Ruben slowed at Michael's door then turned to me with hushed tones. "He's on a call, but he's almost done."

He pushed his way inside and I followed, my heart thumping all the way down to my stomach when I laid eyes on the boss man. That morning, when I'd last seen him, he'd still been in his boxers, hair all mussed up from sleep and our lovemaking. Now he was properly caffeinated and dressed like the billion dollar success that he was. His thick black hair was up in a loose ponytail, keeping it out of his face. Michael was pacing around the room as a voice droned on about something or other over a fancy speakerphone. He smiled as soon as we locked eyes and whatever had popped loose inside of me started to slide back into place.

Ruben sat back down at the large round table that took up one corner of Michael's four bedroom, five bath office, and continued taking notes on the call.

A woman's voice filled the room. "If she accepts, she will be in violation of her contract."

"Let's contact the people at HomeTV and see what we can do. Tabitha has a strong base and it's only growing. I'd like to offer her something that will grow her brand, while being mutually beneficial to Craftsman and HomeTV."

There were affirmative responses on the line, then I didn't know if the meeting was actually over or not, but Michael ended it. Ruben clicked the button on the speakerphone then started gathering up his things.

"Are you going to call it an early day?" he asked looking between us. I shook my head.

"No, I have to get back. I just wanted to stop by."

"'Kay." He excused himself, pausing to give me a parting kiss on the cheek before he slipped out the door.

"Hello," Michael said as he leaned against his desk. He beckoned me closer with a simple lift of his eyebrow. I left my purse on the loveseat by the door and walked into his arms. He pulled me closer, his arms slung low around my waist.

"Come by to share more of your sweet

poetry?"

"No. It's a song this time. It's called 'I Want to Touch Your Butt Sexually.'"

"I hoped you choreographed a dramatic interpretation of the lyrics."

"Of course I did," I said, then I sighed, resting my cheek against his shoulder. He kissed the top of my head.

"What's going on? Talk to me."

"Nothing. I signed the prenup. You're shockingly thorough."

He leaned back a little, forcing me to meet his gaze. "This isn't an out clause for me, Kayla. People get real fucked up when it comes to this type of money. Say something happens and Steven or your family starts encouraging us to play hardball. Or I pass away and my family or even Steven or Holger or Ruben wants to start challenging you for parts of my estate."

"I will fight Holger. Watch me."

"I won't be able to. I'll be dead."

"I'm glad we're keeping this light. So I guess it's official now."

"Yeah, I guess so. We can call our families tonight if you like. Change your Facebook status so it's really official."

"I'm not posting a picture of this." I leaned back a little so we could look at the meteor on my finger together. Then Michael kissed me.

That weirdness, the wobbly bits, faded a little more when our lips touched and even more when his tongue brushed against mine. I figured if our mouths could stay permanently fused together, that shitty feeling would go away completely.

Chapter Five

By the time I left Michael's office it was almost four-thirty and it seemed silly to go back to work. I sent Daniella a text letting her know that I'd be back in the office in the morning. Maybe by then I'd have gotten up the nerve to do the really important things like changing my Facebook status to ENGAGED. Oh and maybe I should tell my parents that Michael had actually proposed. Maybe then all of this would feel less surreal. It seemed like there was some sort of law about at least telling your mother within the first twenty-four hours, but everything had happened so quickly and then the celebratory sex and the time difference. I figured Michael and I could call them when he got home.

But the universe wasn't done gently tripping me up the stairs. The second I walked in the door— I didn't even get a full minute to enjoy the attack of puppy cuddles that was waiting for me—Michael called. The league had officially processed his offer of purchase, a cool one billion dollars to make it real. They wanted him in Miami the following morning for his first press conference and he wanted me there with him. Like I'd told him, I was game. I was down. Team Bradbury-Davis, ready, break! Or was it just Team Bradbury now? Either way, I took a minute to enjoy the fact that Holger had taught Patch how to sit and then I quickly packed my things. I grabbed some stuff for Michael, then loaded Penny and Patch in the Suburban so PJ could take us to pick up Michael and Ruben from their office. I texted Daniella again on the way.

Change of plans. It's going down tonight. Leaving for Miami now.

She hit me back right away.

How exciting! Have fun and tell Michael I said good luck.

I wish you could come. I realized that nonsensical feeling of ickiness was back as I typed the words. I really needed to get it together.

Duke is still on time out. I can't risk running into him out in those streets. You know what I mean. Next time, though.

She sent a few heart emojis and that was that. I'd be with Michael and the puppies and Ruben, but somehow I still felt like I was on my own, which didn't make sense. I didn't realize how loud I'd groaned until I caught PJ looking at me in the rearview mirror.

"I'm fine. Just forgot something. Nothing important though."

He glanced at me again, keeping his focus on the road and just nodded. PJ never said much.

When Michael hopped in the car he paused mid-conversation with Ruben to kiss me and greet the dogs and then it was back to business. They talked Miami and all the other business odds and ends he had to move around now that the deal was really happening.

The flight crew was ready for us when we got to the airport and after waiting our turn for clearance we were on our way. I sat on the couch with Michael, holding the puppies, keeping them distracted and secure during take off while Ruben gave us more of the low-down on what to expect when we arrived in Florida.

"The house is good to go. I already called ahead to the owner and I've arranged for a housekeeper who cooks and is good with walking the dogs. Her name is Vera. Holger actually found her so I'm sure you guys'll love her. Aaaand … Paola Morre just sent over your full schedule for tomorrow." Ruben did some pressing and some sliding on his tablet before he went on.

"Okay. Let's see. The announcement will be made in two hours. We can watch online. She sent a link. OMG Paola, so considerate. The press conference is at ten a.m. at The Continental Hotel, but they would like us there at nine a.m., then there will be a full press junket with Coach Bata, Kevin Mal and Derek Chekovick. All the local papers and a bunch of sports journalists will be there…" He trailed off before he looked up at Michael. "Looks like that will take up the rest of the afternoon, but I'll have lunch brought for you. You have dinner with Mr.

Sands, Rick Chase and Coach Bata tomorrow night. Kayla, we can hit South Beach if you want," he added with a smile.

"Su—"

"I'd like you to come along, actually," Michael said.

"Um, Sands has asked for no significant others," Ruben replied. "This time around. But Coach Bata has invited you both over for breakfast on Sunday, so you can meet his wife and their kids."

I looked over at Michael as a muscle flexed along his bearded jaw. I knew what he was thinking. He was weighing what he wanted against not pissing off his new colleagues.

"It's fine, baby. We'll meet you right after, right?"

"Yeah we can grab a bite and hang nearby," Ruben suggested. I was glad we were on the same page. Didn't feel right to split up the team.

"Fine," Michael said, eventually. "What's on deck for Friday?"

"God, this took forever. It's the second to last game of the regular season. They have a family and fans day on the books already. Two dozen or so parents get to bring their kids to meet and greet and shoot around with the players. They'd like you to be there for that. And then you'll say a few words before tip off. I almost said the coin toss. This is crazy!"

"It is pretty cool," I added.

"Well let's just hope it stays cool and I don't regret it," Michael added. He was a perfectionist. His crankiness was perfection based.

Ruben went on laying out the rest of the weekend and the month. Miami had made it to the play-offs so the season wasn't over. More games, more events. We would be busy. I'd have to figure something out with Daniella. They went back to talking non-sporty business as Sandy served us dinner. The puppies passed out, lulled to sleep by the hum of the engines and me? I was just restless.

I'd been so busy with K&D, I'd almost forgotten just how packed Michael's schedule was when he didn't have the responsibility of a professional sports franchise. We watched the announcement from the league commissioner, Laurence Stockton. It was an excessively long press conference just to say that the team had been sold and Michael would be speaking the next day. He took a few questions, talking Michael up and bringing the focus back to the players and fans with every answer, refusing to comment on the charges against John Taylor Wayne.

We all seemed to relax a little once it was over, but that was only the tip of the iceberg. Michael and Ruben's phones started ringing. I leaned over and kissed Michael on his cheek.

"I'm going to go call my mom."

He glanced at the number flashing across his screen before he looked at me. "Everything okay?"

"Yeah. I just—" I held up my hand and waggled my ring finger. "I haven't told her yet."

"Shit. Let's call her together." The call went to voicemail, but his phone immediately started to ring again. This time it was his nephew, Mitchell.

"No, no, you're fine. Talk to Mitch. I'll be quick. I think we need to have our mother-daughter chat anyway. Get the dress ball rolling."

He gave my fingers a slight squeeze. "Okay."

"I'll be back in a minute." I walked to the back of the plane and closed the bedroom door behind me. My mom had just finished cleaning up from dinner when she picked up the phone. She was happy for me and so were the twins who I could hear shouting their hellos in the background. My dad said his quick congrats and let me know that Michael had done the honorable thing by asking his permission. I teased him a bit, reminding him that this wasn't the sixties anymore. My dad agreed, pulling absolutely no punches, and said that he would happily let Michael pay for the wedding since we were being all modern and what not. And then my mom did the one thing I never thought she'd do. She cried.

"I was worried about you, but you know that."

"Yes, ma'am."

"But you always call me when something's bothering you or when something isn't right, big or small, and I haven't heard one bad word out of your mouth about Michael."

"He's a good man, mom. He loves me a lot."

"I know he does, honey. I know he does. I'm praying for you both."

Despite what I'd told Michael, I admitted I was a little too overwhelmed to talk particulars. Too tired to talk dresses and bridesmaids and preliminary guest lists, but we would and soon. After we hung up I thought about going back out to the main cabin to join the guys for the rest of the flight, but instead I changed my Facebook relationship status to ENGAGED, grabbed one of the spare throw blankets from the storage cabinets, and then I went to sleep.

When I woke up, the lights in the cabin were dimmed and Michael was in the bed with me. I didn't remember him coming in and joining the slumber party, but there he was on top of the suede comforter, his arm draped around my waist when Sandy knocked and let us know we were making our approach.

As soon as we landed in Miami, we headed to the house we'd be living in until we bought our own place. Michael was not playing when he said it was humid, holy shit. I could taste the equator the minute we stepped off the plane. We were only in the heat for six minutes before we got in the air-conditioned car, but it was enough to make me drowsy again. It was only five a.m. and my body was very much still on west coast time.

Our driver, Emmanuel, dropped Ruben off at his hotel. He just wanted to check in and shower, and then he'd be over to our new place to join Michael for the rest of his day. We only had a little over two hours before Michael had to be on his way to the press conference. Thinking about how much caffeine I would need to get through this day, I watched the city go by as we drove to this ridiculous mansion on the water. I'm talking ridiculous. Michael's house was big in that "big for a single guy" type of way. This place was too big for four families of four.

Vera, a tall, slim, extremely tight, older Eastern European woman, was waiting for us by the front door with two sets of keys. I thought we'd have a female version of Holger to deal with, but she was much sweeter and way less bossy. I still missed our big German though. She took the dogs off our hands and suggested we have a look around while Emmanuel brought our bags inside.

We made it through three of the eight bedrooms before we found the master suite. It had HIS and HERS everything. I came out of the HERS bathroom that was attached to the HERS "dressing closet" and met Michael by the huge bed that was up on this raised platform. The look on his face matched mine.

"What was Ruben thinking? We don't need all this."

"I think this was a recommendation from the GM's office. I'm sure new players want something over the top when they sign."

"And they thought you had to show out too? When we move we should downsize. Why didn't Ruben stay here with us?"

"So he can mentally clock out. We should call my parents."

"Oh. Now?" It was barely six a.m. by that point.

"Yeah. This week has been a little crazy and I'm

sure it's not going to slow down. We should have called them already. Plus they are both early birds."

"Okay." I sat on the bed, swallowing my nerves as Michael fished his tablet out of his bag.

Thanks to his parents' close relationship, his dad noticed early on when his mom started exhibiting the early stages of Alzheimer's, just a few weeks before Michael and I started dating. Michael didn't talk about it often, but they had done everything they could to help her. Medications, exercise, hiring additional help around the house to assist both of his aging parents, everything they could do to make her comfortable. Though she was showing more signs of the disease as time went on, Myra and Matthew shared that she still had plenty of good days, but that that didn't mean she was suddenly back to normal. I was hesitant to wonder whether this was going to be a good day or bad day, or if we were going to be able to talk to her at all.

Michael sat down beside me on the bed as he brought up "Mom & Dad" on the video chat app and hit send. My parents had always seemed like the big hurdle, but that didn't mean I didn't want Michael's parents to like me and it definitely didn't mean I wasn't afraid they wouldn't be too keen on us getting married. His parents were born in an era where interracial marriage came with jail time.

The tablet made its little bubbling ring noise twice before the screen lit up with the top of Herbert Bradbury's head.

"Oh, wait. Look. I think I've got it," he said as his face came into full view. "There we are. Good morning!" He was sporting the biggest smile. Michael's dad was glow-in-the-dark white, with white hair that still had wisps of blond around his temples. Michael had gotten the shape of his face and his bright blue eyes from his father, but that was pretty much it. The rest was all his mom.

"Come, have a seat, Nina. Come say hello to Kayla. Hi Kayla," Herbert said.

"Hello," I said, smiling wide.

Michael's mom slid into the frame. She was not so cheery as she made herself comfortable. She was in her early seventies, but she looked great. Her lightly tanned skin was still tight and her hair was a beautiful mixture of black and grey. Michael had her mouth and her nose. "Michael, tell your father I don't need a nurse. Especially not a man nurse," she said with a hint of an accent, maybe British.

"Gregory has been very helpful and I think he should stay," Herbert said.

"I agree with your husband. How are you feeling today, mom?" Michael asked.

"I'm fine. I've been fine. Stop with all the fussing. Tell them, Herbert. I've been having a good week."

"She has. She's trying a new medication that seems to be helping. And I am learning how to cook."

"What about Melba?" Michael asked. I peeked over at the frown creasing Michael's eyebrows.

"Melba's here. She's making breakfast right now. I was just feeling a little useless around here. You got us this wonderful home and all this help, I thought I'd learn some of your mum's favorite dishes." It was hard to see clearly, but I was pretty sure Herbert reached up and rubbed the back of Michael's mom's neck. So that's where he got it from.

"Married a half century and he still loves me. Now let me see." Even after the vaguely self-deprecating dig, I felt myself smiling wider as she tilted the screen so she could get a better look at us. I had a feeling there was a pair of her reading glasses around their house somewhere.

"Kayla."

"Yes, ma'am."

"Yes, Herbert shows me your picture every day. I'd remember those dimples anywhere."

"I'm glad I finally get to see you guys," I replied. God, they weren't even my parents and I felt terrible about not visiting them.

"When Michael told me he was going to propose, I thought it was a little too good to be true," Herbert said. "And then I find out I get a new daughter-in-law and a new set of season tickets all in one week. I believe I understand how to purchase a basketball team, but you have to tell us how you wooed this beautiful young lady."

"The old Bradbury charm," Michael said with a little chuckle.

"He tricked with me with all his kindness and consideration. I tried to resist it, but I failed," I said.

"Kayla, I'd like to say it's all a ruse, but he's always been my sweetest child."

"I won't tell Myra that," I said.

We chatted a little bit longer about how they were happy that Michael was finally settling down and how maybe we should think about getting married in Michigan since Michael never does anything in Michigan. Soon someone I assumed was Gregory, the male nurse, popped in to let them know that Melba had prepared a delicious breakfast for Nina. Nina let him know she wasn't a child and would be down when she felt like eating. We hung up with them then, promising to come visit after the NBA Finals were over.

It was a little surreal. I was about to have in-laws.

Michael placed the tablet on the bed, then leaned forward scrubbing his face. He was exhausted.

"I'm glad both our folks know now. I'm sorry we didn't call them sooner," he said.

"I changed my Facebook status last night. I'm afraid to check my phone." I eyed my purse that was sitting on the floor. There were a bunch of unread texts I was avoiding too. It was too early in the morning to be this overwhelmed. I looked up when Michael's warm hand slid around the back of my neck. I leaned into his touch.

"Are you alright?" he asked.

"Yeah, I'm fine. Why?"

"Just wondering." He kissed my forehead.

"Does your mom have any brown in her?" I half teased. "She looks too good for her age not to."

"She's half Indian."

"Oh that explains why you're not all the way square," I said as I bumped his side.

"Yeah, that one quarter really saved me. She met my dad while he was traveling in Europe. He thought his draft number would get called so he went backpacking just in case Vietnam was the last place he got to see."

"Glad things worked out differently there."

"You're not the only one. You don't have to come to the press conference. You can stay here and rest."

"No, I want to come. I'm gonna be dead around four, but it's fine. We have a slow morning tomorrow. We'll catch up on sleep then. I don't know if I can sleep now anyway. I'm too keyed up."

"Do you want me to help you sleep?"

I looked over at him as his hand moved down my back. The last twenty-four hours I felt like I'd been walking on marbles and the way I saw it, I wouldn't be back on stable flooring for a while, but that look on his face, the look in his eyes, it swept all the chaos away.

"I think I could use a *little* help." I lay back on the giant bed that didn't belong to us. Michael took the invitation and leaned over me, kissing my lips all soft and slow. My pussy swelled instantly, just from the weight of his body on me. Everything was off, a little fucked up with the temporary move and the team and the prenup, but this felt perfect. The button on my jeans was flicked open with ease and then his hand was inside my underwear. My thighs pressed together, then eased apart as his hand moved lower.

"I think if we start by getting you out of these clothes…" I squeezed my eyes closed as two of his fingers moved over my clit. "Or do you want to keep your clothes on?" And then those same two fingers pushed inside of me. I grabbed his wrist and held on as I licked my lips. His hard-on was moving against my hip.

"I want you," I moaned.

And then we were interrupted. The doorbell rang, but it wasn't just the doorbell. It sounded like a doorbell's chimes echoing through forty-eight megaphones lined up ass to mouth. We both jumped at the bone shaking sound.

"Fuck." Michael slumped forward, rubbing his face against my shoulder. "I had Ruben arrange for a shape up before the press conference. That's probably the barber."

"I don't care who it is. That doorbell, babe. That has got to go."

Michael smiled a bit, his mustache tipping up and then he wiggled his fingers, making my cunt clench on his hand. "You want me to make him wait?"

The doorbell rang again, making my teeth vibrate. "No. Please. Vera must still be out with the dogs. Please let him in."

Michael laughed and kissed me again as he pulled his hand out of my jeans. This week needed to end. I wanted my boyfriend back. My fiancé. I glared at him as he stood, then licked his fingers clean as he backed toward the bedroom's massive door.

"You're nasty."

"I know. That's why you're marrying me. I'll have Vera talk to the owners. Take a nap. Take a shower. Come down when you're ready."

"'Kay. I love you."

"I love you, too."

Chapter Six

I needed a shower for sure, but a shower turned out to be a horrible idea. Ten seconds under the hot spray and I was ready for a serious nap. I got out of the shower and lay down on the bed, and I woke up thirty minutes later groggy as hell and even more confused because I didn't recognize the room I was in. It didn't help that the sound of that god-awful doorbell was what ripped me from my sleep.

Some sweet person had brought my luggage up. I brushed my teeth and changed into this houndstooth dress I bought to wear somewhere special. I grabbed a new pair of black wedge ankle boots out of my suitcase and a little black jacket to match. As soon as I woke all the way up I would appreciate just how cute I looked. In desperate need of food before I did anything else, I made my way downstairs toward the sound of Ruben's echoing laughter. The house really was big as hell for no good reason.

The kitchen/great room was hopping with activity. Ruben was on the couch with some woman I didn't know. She was Latina, I think—only one of my eyes was all the way open. They were playing with Patch while Penny snoozed at Ruben's feet. Another black woman I didn't know seemed to be putting a whole MAC kiosk full of makeup out on the counter.

Vera was busy at the stove. It looked like she was making breakfast for twice the number of people. Julius, Michael's barber, was there finishing up his handiwork on Michael's beard. I felt like a little kid who had just woken up from a nap during their parents' dinner party. I was still so sleepy, in a half haze, I just walked directly toward Michael. He was the most familiar thing in the room.

"Good morning." I managed to squeak out. I was greeted by a round of hellos and good mornings in return.

"If it ain't Miss Thicka-Than-A-Snicka," Julius said with his deep laugh.

"Hi Jules." I gave him a half hug and a kiss on the cheek and then I leaned over and kissed Michael's lips. He reached out and squeezed my hand.

"Kayla, this is Paola from the GM's office. And Zia, who is here to do your hair and makeup," Ruben explained.

"Hi, good morning," I tried again. "I'm sorry I'm out of it. I hit like half a REM cycle and now I feel like I got hit by a bus. Is there coffee?"

"There sure is," Vera said, with her thick accent, nodding to a little coffee machine on the far counter.

"Thank you. Zia, do you mind if we eat first? I'll be way less twitchy once I'm fed."

"Absolutely," she replied. "And I hear congrats are in order."

"Huh?" I looked down at Michael as he squeezed my hand then rotated my engagement ring a little. "Oh, thank you. It's all pretty fresh."

"Lemme see." I cringed a little as Zia made that flapping come-over-here gesture with her hand, mostly 'cause I'd just met her and mostly 'cause I'd always been a little weirded out by overly familiar strangers. I tried to smile when Zia complimented the ring and then made my way over to Paola so she could ogle the diamond too.

"Have you guys set a date?" Paola asked.

"No, not yet," I replied.

"My man was smart. Locked that shit down real quick."

I shook my head, laughing a bit. "Shut up, Jules."

"I'm just saying. I know more than a few boys at the shop who are still jealous."

"Yeah, yeah. You came all the way down here to shape him up?" Julius had a barbershop up in Harlem. During Michael's monthly trips to New York he stopped in to get a trim. I usually tagged along, and loved getting to know Julius and the other guys who ran the shop. Michael was one of his favorite customers, but Miami seemed a bit far down I-95 for fifteen minutes worth of work.

"Hell nah. Your newly acquired power forward, Kyrie Willis? That's my nephew. I was coming down here to visit him when your boy called."

"Ah okay."

"I was just telling Michael about everything we have planned over the next few days," Paola said. Clearly I'd interrupted something. I took the hint and clammed up. I made myself a cup of coffee while

Paola went back to rehashing the schedule Ruben had gone over with us during our flight. I made myself comfortable in one of the high chairs next to Zia.

"You're on social media, right Kayla?" Paola asked out of the blue.

"Um, yeah I'm on Facebook and Instagram. I have a Twitter, but I never use it much."

"Well we set up accounts for Mr. Bradbury. The fans love interacting with the whole team, including the owner."

"Oh okay." I smiled and nodded, keeping my comments on how Wayne's interactions with fans had landed him in a rather pickle of a jam. "Yeah, he's not big on using social media for himself, but Ruben and I will show him the ropes."

"And if not, just let us know. We can have someone handle tweets and posts for him. Whatever you prefer, sir."

I looked up at Michael as he stood and let Julius sweep the loose hairs off his shoulders. "I think between the three of us, we can handle it."

Vera served breakfast and once my coffee kicked in, I hopped in Zia's chair and let her get my face and my hair together. We agreed on lashes. I hate doing them myself, but when someone else has to fiddle with the glue they are totally worth it. After Michael showered and dressed, we said bye to the puppies and Vera and Julius, then piled into the SUVs waiting for us. Zia had apparently been hired to get Michael camera ready, but after he declined anything more than a little anti-shine powder on his forehead, Ruben suggested she stick around to touch up my makeup throughout the day.

Michael was the focus, but if I was going to be with him I would surely end up on camera and a girl's gotta look her best. After the mist of my morning nap wore off I realized how smart of a move that was. As we got closer to The Continental Hotel, my hands started shaking. Too little sleep, too much caffeine. Oh and Michael had just purchased a basketball team. I'd have mascara all over my cheek if I were left to do it myself.

Knowing Michael needed a few minutes to gather his thoughts, Ruben kept Zia and Paola occupied, asking them about the good spots to eat and clubs we could check out while we were in town. I wondered how long we would be in town. Six months out of the year? Ten? Would it even make sense for us to keep a place in L.A.? Miami seemed cool. Too hot to breathe, but like Malibu, I liked the feel of being on the water. But did I want to live there for good? Did Michael? Another discussion to table for another time.

With those kinds of easy breezy thoughts running through my head, I figured it might be time to check my phone. I had a bunch of messages and comments on Facebook, congratulating us on our engagement, and one annoying "To who??" comment from a girl I hadn't talked to since middle school. I had a few missed calls and voicemails, and a dozen or so texts. The first was from my dad.

Michael bought The Flames?!? I almost snorted as I sent him a text back.

Yes. Your first grandchild is an NBA franchise. Congrats.

Too old to be a grandpa. I look too good. But good for him. Smart move.

I shook my head as I clicked over to a text from my cousin. He just wanted to make sure the guy I brought to Thanksgiving was the same guy who just bought Miami. I assured him they were one and the same.

The smile on my face faded when I saw the next text was from my old roommate, Adler. We'd still be friends if she hadn't groped Michael and tried to get between us.

I looked at her *Congrats. I'm really happy for you guys. Seriously* for a few long moments before moving on to my email. Gordo sent me a virtual bouquet of flowers and then demanded that we get together as soon as possible so he could grill me. I also got a sweet email from Monica at Arrangements, expressing her excitement at our ultimate love connection. She was one of the few people who actually knew that Michael had started off as my Sugar Daddy. Hopefully she'd continue to keep that information to herself. There was an e-card from my first college roommate, and Daniella emailed over links to hideous bridesmaids dresses under the subject line LET US NOT. And then there was an email from Sarah McNamara with an attachment. I knew it was stupid, but that feeling came back, that vile feeling that made me want to tug at my own skin. I signed the thing. Michael signed the thing. Why was she emailing me? I cringed as I opened it.

Good morning Ms. Davis, attached is a copy of the prenuptial agreement between you and Mr. Michael Bradbury. A hard copy, signed by both parties will be delivered to your Malibu residence later today. Please feel free to contact me with any further questions.

And please congratulate Mr. Bradbury on his recent acquisition. My husband is a big fan.

Under different circumstances I would probably like Sarah McNamara. I didn't touch the attachment. I told myself there was no need to. We'd been engaged for eight whole minutes and had spent maybe thirty-seven seconds of that eight minutes acknowledging the good news to each other as a couple. There was no way I was going to spend another moment thinking about what would happen if we got divorced. I locked my phone instead and dropped it into my purse. Then I decided comparing the difference between Florida palm trees and California palm trees was a great way to keep myself preoccupied while Michael silently rehearsed his remarks.

When we got to The Continental, there was a tiny swarm of paparazzi waiting by the front entrance. Paola hopped out of the SUV and led the way through the chaos. Michael took my hand and I followed him through the barrage of flashes and questions about the charges against the former owner. Inside we were ushered toward some conference rooms and that's when we were separated. Michael was handed off to some other member of the team's staff. He kissed me quickly on the temple then disappeared through another set of doors with Zia on his heels. Paola took Ruben and I to a green room where we could watch the press conference.

Two monitors were set up opposite a large sitting area. A few other people buzzed around the room, but ignored us as we sat down. The feed was already live, showing the table draped with the Miami banner, which was set up with five mics and a half podium. You could see the tops of the heads of members of the press as they chatted amongst themselves and took their seats.

I thought we'd have a second to breathe before it started, but I was wrong. The door swung open as soon as we sat down.

"Where is the Mrs. To-Be!?" A plain-faced, but spectacularly dressed white woman with brown hair nearly shrieked as she entered the room. She was carrying a giant basket loaded down with Miami Flames stuff, and she had a white gift bag stuffed full with green tissue paper dangling from her fingers.

Ruben and I looked at each other. I frowned and then it hit us both.

"You might be looking for me?"

"The future Mrs. Bradbury? Hi! I'm Kate. On behalf of the whole Miami Flames organization, I'd like to say welcome to Miami."

"Thank you."

"Come on over here. Let me show you what we got."

I gave Ruben the look, you know the one, then followed Kate over to the table where they'd laid out some refreshments. Quick on her feet, Paola jumped up and moved a tray of bagel halves over before Kate accidentally knocked them on the floor. I thanked her before facing the basket.

Kate started pointing out all sorts of stuff with the Flames logo on it. Mugs, a teddy bear that I knew the dogs would destroy if they got their paws on it. But then Kate pointed out a little bag of dog biscuits and two rubber bones, because of course she'd heard we had two new puppies. Flames cellphone cases and two tins of Flames mints. There were t-shirts, two hoodies, a fleece throw blanket, and a small envelope filled with coupons to spas and restaurants around town. There were free movie passes in there too.

And then she held up the white gift bag. "This is for you." She waggled her eyebrows at me and I was suddenly terrified to stick my hand in the bag. Luckily, just as I thanked her, Paola saved the day.

"Oh they're about to start. Thank you, Kate."

"No problem!" She finger waved, then did this sort of odd sideways, backward shuffle out the door.

I brought the gift bag back over to the couch and shoved my hand inside. Now that Kate was gone I wouldn't have to temper my reaction. My knuckles hit what turned out to be a pink glittery bath bomb. There was a gift certificate for a free in-home massage and mani/pedi and a Tiffany bracelet with a heart charm engraved with "MRS." Rolled to the side was a black Flames jersey. I pulled it out of the bag and looked at the back. MRS. BRADBURY and the number two were stitched in white lettering into the black fabric. I didn't have to look at the tag to confirm that something was very wrong, but I rotated it anyway and looked at the XS staring back at me.

Ruben covered his mouth and just barely hid his cackle. I stared back at him.

"Did nobody tell these people how fat I am?"

"Oh my god, stop. We'll get you one that's the right size."

"Fuck that. I'm wearing this and a g-string on our honeymoon. It's just enough fabric to cover my nipples."

"I'm sure he'll love that. Can we have this stuff sent to the house?" Ruben asked Paola.

"Of course.

"Thank you," I said to him.

"What? Were you supposed to carry that big ass thing around all day?" he said, pointing to the gift basket.

"Kate seems to think so."

Finally someone I actually knew appeared on the screen. Richard Sands, from the commissioner's office, came out to the podium and introduced himself, then explained how the presser would go. He would introduce Michael, who would have a few minutes to say what he wanted to say and then they would hear from a few of the players and the coach. There would be a Q&A, but they would take absolutely no questions about the ongoing investigation. The team co-captains Kevin Mal and Derek Chekovick, Coach Bata and the general manager, Rick Chase, came out first and then Michael. My stomach fluttered for him. He was cool as could be, but I was filled with secondhand anxiety.

Coach Bata didn't have much to say, but Kevin and Derek said some very nice things about Michael coming in and basically saving the day. There were some jokes about him passing the criminal background check. Then it was Michael's turn to speak. I watched his every movement as he moved his mic closer. All the exhaustion and introspection that had hung all over him during the ride over was gone.

"I'd like to thank Richard and the commissioner's office for looking the other way on some of the more shady items on that background check." And of course everyone laughed.

"They love him," Ruben said under his breath.

"No, we've found ourselves in a very unique situation. I'm thankful for the opportunity to support this organization and these players. This was all very sudden and unexpected—" Kevin Mal said something, but was out of range of the mic. Everyone within earshot of the first two rows laughed though.

"Yeah, this wasn't planned," Michael went on.

"But this is life, you know. Horrible things happen and sometimes all you can do is move on, hopefully with better, stronger pieces in place. I'm looking forward to getting to know the guys and supporting them through the end of their season. And I'm looking forward to working with Rick and Coach Bata as they prepare for next season. What's important now is that the team doesn't lose their momentum. I want them to finish strong and not have to worry about what's going on in the owner's box."

"God, how is he so calm," I muttered. "I'd be shaking."

"You know him. He lives for this shit. Not the on-camera shit, but he lives for the art of the deal and they just made it so much sweeter by throwing basketball into the mix."

"I know, but still. I have no idea how he's so cool under pressure. It drives me crazy."

The Q&A was relatively short since the focus was on just introducing Michael. Paola explained that Kevin and Derek would be back in front of the cameras the following night after the game to talk more about the team. Kevin presented Michael with a Flames jersey with BRADBURY and the number one on the back. From the look of things he'd be able to fit that jersey over his torso. Richard wrapped things up and it was over. I finally let out the breath I'd been holding in my stomach.

"God, that was awful. I feel like I was nervous for the both of us."

"I'm glad you guys met. You're so good for

him," Ruben said as he gave my hand a light squeeze. "Are you excited?"

"In theory. I can't really think about it." I flicked my wrist, motioning around the room. "More pressing things and what not."

"I understand. He'll get a break soon. I'll make sure I schedule it in."

"Thank you."

A few moments later, Michael came back in the green room. He handed the jersey to Ruben. "I have to head upstairs. Come on."

The rest of the morning was a weird repetitive blur. We moved from room to room, Team Bradbury and his entourage, while Michael was interviewed one on one by various news outlets. Michael charmed the pants off everyone, even the one ass who asked several times in various ways how someone who made their fortune in dating websites was qualified to own a team. Michael shot back, rattling off several instances of owners who owned movie theater chains and casinos.

"The thing we all have in common is people. I'm here for the players and fans, to anticipate their needs and to help fix the things that aren't working. That's how I made my billions. That's why I'm qualified."

Ruben pressed his lips to my shoulder to keep

his "Yaasssss bitch" under control. I clenched both my lips between my teeth.

We broke for lunch around one. I was able to steal one kiss before Michael and Ruben spent the next thirty minutes going over all the emails that had come through over the course of the morning. Only half of them had to do with basketball. Paola seemed to be catching up on work of her own as her fingers moved across her phone. Daniella texted me though, giving me a sense of purpose once again.

Just got to the office and Lili found this. There was a link and a laughing smiley face. I clicked the url to the popular gossip site, TheDish.com.

I laughed at the headline: MIAMI FLAMES HAVE A NEW OWNER AND HE'S FREAKING HOT

Michael and Ruben both glanced up at me, but I waved them off. I scrolled down and read through the hilarious article talking about how Michael's "daddy good looks" would do wonders for the team and the NBA overall. He was exactly what the league needed for female and gay fans alike to take the game seriously again.

And then they included what looked like every picture they could find of Michael with captions like "This is the ruggedly sexy beard of a man who makes sound business decisions" and "These eyes, the color of a bottomless lagoon, are the eyes of a man who increases your profit margins." I recognized a few of the more candid pictures mostly because I'd been cropped out of them, but I didn't care. It was still pretty funny. She sent me a few more links 'cause the Internet takes like five seconds to scent eligible bachelor chum in the water, but I didn't get to look at all of them.

Michael had two more interviews before he got a short break, but I knew he would take that time to change and regroup before he went out to dinner with Coach Bata and company.

He sat down with a feature writer from FirstQuarter.Com. The first thing out of her mouth threw us all off, all of us but Michael.

"Let me start by saying congratulations. I heard that you were recently engaged."

I leaned back in my chair, a little stunned, but Michael just smiled like he'd been waiting for the question all day. "Ah yes. Thank you. Her name's Kayla and she's actually with us right now." The reporter turned around and looked at Paola who was sitting beside me. And then she looked at Zia who was standing by the door.

I threw her a bone and gave a little wave. My whole face was heating up. "Hi."

"Oh, hi! Congrats!" She didn't hide the surprise in *her* voice very well.

"Thank you," I said, trying not to hurl. She spared me any further embarrassment and got back to the interview at hand. As they talked some about the growth in Michael's career and why team ownership was even on his radar, Daniella shot me another text.

Welp that didn't take very long. With it she sent me the link to a tweet from The Dish.

Noooo! @MichaelBrd_bury is engaged!

There was a gif of Carlton from Fresh Prince screaming. Then another text popped up from Daniella.

Is your Instagram set to private?

The hurl. It was rising.

Chapter Seven

A girl from the twins' school sold me out. Some boys on the bus were talking about the team changing ownership. Some girl overheard and looked up the story online while she was talking to a friend of Kiara's who also happened to be friends with me on Facebook and Instagram 'cause I'd known her since she was five and she was sweet and she always helped the twins with their chores so they could get back to hanging out faster.

She was sixteen and lived in rural North Carolina and even though my boyfriend was rich, my life was pretty boring so I wasn't sharing anything that would be off the charts interesting to her. She'd been on my page recently, liking all sorts of pictures that I'd posted of the puppies, but why wouldn't she look at my other pictures?

I'd looked at all her pictures once. She was a cheerleader. She had a kinda cute, kinda ugly boyfriend who ran track with Kaleigh. She loved her grandma and De'Bonay. And she remembered seeing a few pictures of me with Michael. So she showed the girl from the bus, who showed the boys from the bus and then the girl from the bus caught my sweet, trusting, unassuming Kiara in the hallway for confirmation, who called me crying right before Michael's last interview, saying that she was so, so sorry but Tae Brown—that was the little snitch's name—had tweeted The Dish over and over until they took her news of our engagement seriously.

They harvested half my Instagram and the few pictures I'd posted of us on Facebook. I didn't say anything about it to Michael right away because other than doing something reactionary and dickish like threatening the gossip sites with a lawsuit, there's wasn't much we *could* do. Mostly because nothing particularly bad had happened. The only reaction in this case was no action. Still, the invasion of privacy—even though, I know, I know, the pictures were public—just added another layer of crap to the weird, shitty way I was already feeling.

I should have known that Michael was up on the whole situation. Very little happened in his universe without him having at least an inkling. As soon as we dropped Ruben off at his hotel he turned to me.

"How are you holding up?" His warm hand brushed my temple then slid down my arm. I didn't want to be touched just then, but I didn't move away.

For some reason, I couldn't look at him when I answered. "I'm fine. Just tired."

"I'm sure you saw this. I saw you typing like mad on your phone." He tilted his cell toward me and showed me the revised post from The Dish, saying he wasn't a free man.

"Yeah. I saw it. Daniella sent me the link. Some girl from the twins' school was nice enough to provide them with the photos."

"Are you upset that people know?"

"No. Are you?"

"Not in the slightest. This is just how the gossip cycle goes. My purchasing the team was actually pretty big news outside of the world of sports. It's not shocking that people dug into who I am and who you are. Some actual celebrity will do something stupid over the weekend and we'll be old news by Monday."

I changed the subject before I sarcastically screamed "Oh! Okay!" in his face.

"How do you feel about today?" I asked. "It seemed like everyone really liked you."

"I think it went very well, all things considered. The fact that I'm not out hiring contract killers helps. I have some new things to think about, things to consider in terms of making positive changes for the team, but it's all good." He smiled at me, still after the longest day ever, calm as can be. I kinda wanted to choke him.

My annoyance was displaced, but it was like a heat-seeking missile and he was the closest warm body, the one person in my life who generated the most heat. I leaned up and kissed him instead, feeling confident that my brain might actually be broken.

Vera had dinner ready for me when we got back to the Manse of Excess. I ate while Michael showered and changed. Ruben and I were going to hit a club, but as soon my meal settled in my stomach my whole body declared it was done for the day.

I collapsed on the couch with Penny and sent Ruben a text.

I can't. Too sleepy. You can't make me.

He must have reached the same conclusion at the very same moment because his response was lightning fast.

Oh thank god. I'm getting room service and knocking out. We have more meetings in the morning. I need rest. Ruben needs rest!

"Great," I muttered out loud. "So much for that a.m. quality time." I dropped my phone and picked up the remote to the jumbo television. Just as I figured out how to get the cable to work, Michael came walking into the living area with Patch trailing behind him. I clicked my teeth for him to come join Penny and me on the couch.

"How do I look?" Michael asked. He looked great. The dark grey suit and the light blue shirt worked well together and his slicked back hair made him look downright fuckable.

"How are you so perky and alert right now. Are you on speed? You can tell me."

Michael laughed as he leaned over the arm of the couch to kiss me. "No, baby. I can't say that I am. Let me get going."

"I'll see you Sunday night some time?"

"Hilarious. I'll be back by eleven. I'll wake you up for some butt stuff."

"Can't wait." I shouldn't have sighed because then he did that thing. He stood back and looked at me for a second. I was still in my houndstooth dress, my lashes were still glued into place, but I knew what I looked like. I looked like shit and I was sulking.

"Are you okay?" he asked for the fourth time.

And then I did that thing 'cause the answer was obviously no, but his driver was waiting and he had to go out and work so we could afford to do things like stay in a mega mansion in Miami. And the answer wasn't simple. I hadn't even wrapped my mind around the full answer.

It was the day. The whole week. The ring on my finger, and the man who was walking away from me. And not because he didn't love me. He did and I knew it, I felt it every moment we spent together, but he had to go do the things he did best, the things that brought us together in the first place. But the answer was definitely no, I was not fine, I just didn't know why. And how do you open talks and negotiations on an issue you haven't discovered yet.

"Yeah. I'm just sleepy as shit. Ruben and I are going to stay in tonight. We'll South Beach it up another night."

"That sounds like a smart plan." He kissed me again, a few times, on my lips and my cheeks and my lips again. "Get some rest." And then he was gone.

I watched some crap TV, feeling more antsy and restless and overtired with every commercial break. On Vera's assurance that the neighborhood provided a lovely scenic stroll, I took the puppies for their nightly walk. When I got back Vera showed me how to reach her down in the maid's quarters (the fucking house had maid's quarters) if I needed her.

She'd be there the rest of the night. I showered

and changed into my pajamas, then climbed into bed with the dogs and my laptop. Getting any work done was hopeless. I was too tired to be creative, but too anxious to sleep. TV movies seemed like a great idea. The Sex and the City movie was about to start its fiftieth airing that week. I turned to it and ending up catching the tail end of Entertainment News.

"You ladies have been going crazy over this man all day. And some of the fellas," Jay Lance, their one black reporter joked.

"Yes, this week the Miami Flames announced their new owner and today we got the first glimpse of the extremely attractive Michael Bradbury in action," Liza Carino, their star reporter added. They showed a clip of Michael accepting the jersey at the press conference. "Many fans and a few members of our staff were devastated to find out that Bradbury is in fact engaged to graphic designer, Kayla Davis. The two reportedly met when Bradbury turned up to a mixer for AskCupid.com in Los Angeles last June."

"That's a pretty short courtship," the other reporter, Amy Mays, added, like anyone fucking asked her.

"You have to remember that Hollywood operates on dog years," Liza replied. That got a whole round of chuckles. "But yes. Sorry ladies and some gents. Michael Bradbury is taken."

"Good for you, my man. Snagged a basketball team and new fiancée all in one week," Jay said, wrapping the segment up.

"As opposed to an old fiancée?"

"Well you know what I mean. That's all for

tonight. Tomorrow we'll be back with…"

My phone started ringing. I didn't recognize the number so I hit ignore, like I'd been doing all day. And then I did the only next logical thing. I went to the Internet.

Yes, I went to the Internet and I did the only thing that could make things worse. I searched. Every gossip site had posted something about Michael and nearly every gossip site had posted something about me. I knew it would blow over in a matter of days. That's how these things went, but then I saw it.

New Flames Owner met with Racist Tweets Over New Fiancée

I wasn't stupid enough to click on the link. I knew what the post would say and I knew what the tweets would say. I sent the link to Daniella instead.

This was not my agenda for the week.

OMG. What did Michael say?

Don't know if he's seen it. He's out doing businessman things.

Are you okay?

Ehhhhhhh….

Do you want me to come?
Before I could answer.
Nevermind. I'm coming.

I didn't have it in me to lie and say I didn't want her there.

Get off the Internet and go to bed. I'll be there when you wake up.

I did the smart thing then, and took her advice.

I have no idea what time Michael got home, but he did not wake me up for butt stuff. He wasn't there one second, and then he was there and we were spooning, and the next thing I knew it was morning and that doorbell from hell was ringing again, and he was gone. I hid my head under the pillow until I heard voices coming into the bedroom.

"Wake up, Sunshine."

I peeled back the covers and saw Daniella. She sat on the bed beside me, looking all adorable in her sundress and jean jacket like she'd hadn't just spent the last nine hours traveling. Michael was standing by his HIS closet door, putting on his tie. "You have company."

"Hey. Thanks for coming," I croaked.

"We're gonna have a great day, right? We're gonna get some work done. We're gonna take it easy. Maybe relax by the pool."

"I didn't want you to come because I'm suicidal."

"I know. We're gonna shop and go get Cuban food."

"That sounds like a plan. I love you both." Michael kissed me on the lips and then gave Daniella a playful kiss on the forehead. "Stay the hell away from Twitter and don't answer the phone unless it's immediate family. And I think you might want to consider getting a Ruben so you don't have to field strange calls anymore period."

"That's a great idea," Daniella said with a firm nod.

"I'll see you later." Michael kissed me one more time and then he was gone for real.

"So I have good news and bad news," Daniella said. "The bad news is that I looked at some of the tweets and they are just as awful and sorta worse than you'd expect. Lili's been tracking basically everywhere your or Michael's names pop up. But this will go away."

"And the good news?"

"Check this out." Daniella handed me her phone. The browser was open to this blog, The Flow. I'd visited it pretty frequently. It was run by a few young Black and Asian women and they covered gossip and fashion and entertainment. I looked at the headline.

IT'S BEEN 12 HOURS
AND WE LOVE KAYLA DAVIS

They talked about how cute I was and my great fashion sense, how I was buds with De'Bonay and

Duke, and then they talked about K&D and Queer Qards. They snagged the picture of Daniella, Lili and me from our About page on the K&D website. The final line definitely made me smile.

If you ask us, new Flames owner Michael Bradbury sure knows how to pick 'em. We'd marry you too, Kayla.

"See? Good, right?"

"Definitely good."

"And we've gained a bunch of followers and Facebook likes in the last twenty-four hours. Ignore the assholes and enjoy your man and this ridiculous house." She chuckled, looking up at the fifty-foot ceilings.

"I know. I hate this place."

"Well you and Michael won't even know I'm here. I'm staying down in the southeast quadrant. Do you feel better?"

"I do and I'm sorry I kinda panicked. You didn't have to fly all the way here."

"It's not like you're staying in Siberia, and I have cousins here. Lili is so pissed I came without her, but I didn't have time to arrange anything with FedEx so she's gonna go into the office. I promised her next time. Besides I didn't feel like babysitting her. And... I might have made up with Duke."

"Oh?"

"Okay, we haven't *talked* talked yet. But I miss him," she whined. "I just didn't want to talk about all this love shit with him via text. Face to face is better."

"Does he know you're here?"

"Yeah. I sent him the most passive aggressive text before my flight took off. He told me to call him when I got here. But let's pretend I'm one hundred percent here for you right now because you're my best friend and I love you. Let's you and me talk. Do you want to go shopping for wedding dresses today? Get the ball rolling?"

"Ugh, fuck no."

"Why not?"

"I can't even think wedding stuff. Michael and I have to talk."

"Are you having second thoughts?"

"No, absolutely not. Hell no. I'm keeping this man."

"Okay, so what's wrong?"

"I don't know. That's the problem. I've felt so off ever since the prenup thing and with everything that's happened this week, I feel like I can't catch my breath, but he's too busy to talk right now. And then I feel guilty because he works so hard."

"But something is off."

"I think I might be mad at him."

"You don't know?"

I grimaced and shrugged.

"Wait, have you never been pissed at him before?"

I slowly shook my head. "I don't think so."

"Ugh, I'm sure you haven't. He's pretty perfect. And you guys have never had a fight before?"

"I mean, not really. There was the thing with Adler, but he wasn't pissed at me. It was more like we just had a really intense conversation. We've never been pissed at each other. And I swear to god I'm not courting trouble, but I'm just having feelings and emotions, and I don't know how to deal with them."

"Yeah that's tricky. Feelings and emotions are valid. I'm going to tell you what you would tell me."

"I need to talk to him."

"You need to talk to him. Exactly."

"I'll see if he can pencil me in some time next week."

"Stop! You're busy too. You have a life too."

"You're right! And you were saying something about Cuban food!"

Daniella laughed, smacking my arm with the pillow as she nodded toward my HERS bathroom. "Go get ready."

Daniella was just what the doctor ordered. We took the puppies and had a delicious brunch of Cuban food and did some excellent lady bonding. Zia was coming before the family day event to do my makeup. If I was anywhere near Michael I knew I was going to be on camera, so I didn't object one bit. Daniella was pretty sure Duke was going to show up at the game, so she let Zia contour her up a little when she offered. Our gift baskets had been delivered while we were out and all three of us had a good laugh about that extra small jersey.

When we got to the arena, Paola found us and

directed us to where we could find Michael and Ruben. It was tempting to find a corner where Daniella and I could observe and chat, but we threw ourselves into the mix, meeting a bunch of the players and their families, and some of the fans and their kids.

Some of the players' wives were... complete assholes to Daniella and me. Including Kaheem Howard's wife who, when Daniella excused herself to use the restroom, told me to watch her around Michael.

"She's cute, that one. I wouldn't bring her around my man." Yes, infidelity existed, but um no, and also bitch, we just met. Calm down. Kevin Mal's wife, Asia, was super sweet to us though. She was five months pregnant with their second child and she had some very sage advice for me about dealing with all the madness.

"Just focus on yourself and your man and you'll be fine."

Once the game was about to start we found our seats behind the bench and Michael was whisked off to give his speech. They introduced the starting five and then Kevin Mal got the crowd all hyped and introduced Michael.

He wasn't a get-the-crowd-hyped type of guy, but he did his best.

"How's everybody doing tonight?" he asked, and that of course got some thunderous cheers. "Good, good. You know, I love this game," he said.

"I grew up poor in Detroit and all my brother and I had to look forward to was our trips down to the park so we could play three on three with our friends. This sport kept me sane, this sport kept me happy. Basketball kept me alive. Keeping my grades up so I could play basketball helped me get an academic scholarship to a top university. Without basketball I wouldn't be standing here right now."

"I didn't know any of that," Daniella whispered in my ear. I only knew about a fraction of it.

"When I look at all of these guys," he nodded toward the bench, "and when I look at all of you, I know I'm in the right place. We all love this game." The arena went nuts.

"Thank you all for welcoming me and my family to your fine city." He handed the mic off, and high fived and hugged most of the team as he made his way back toward our seats. Security escorted of course.

"How'd I do?" he asked as he slid into his seat beside me.

"They hated you. We should leave now. Save ourselves the embarrassment."

"I mean we can. I promised you something last night. Something of the butt variety."

"Yeah and you didn't deliver so you're gonna sit here and watch four quarters of this basketball you loooove so much." I was totally joking. I wanted to watch the game too, but I might have had a bit of an attitude.

He flashed his rare wicked smile then leaned over me toward Daniella. "Am I in trouble?"

"Listen, man," she said with a laugh. "I just order the card stock and deal with vendors. You're gonna have to speak to my boss."

He pulled me closer with his arm around my shoulder and kissed me on the head and then he whispered, "I love you even though you're angry with me."

"I have no idea what you're talking about. Let's watch the game." I wasn't angry at him, but him thinking I was only made me feel shittier. I decided to focus on the action on the court instead of whatever weirdness was swirling through my mind.

Duke showed up halfway through the first quarter and that was it for Daniella. I couldn't hear what he was saying to her, but she was still just as smitten as ever, giggling and leaning into him. Stealing kisses and shit. I have no clue how they didn't end up on the Kiss Cam. I couldn't blame her. Duke was a mega star and hot to boot and even though they were having issues it was clear that he felt something strong for her.

The Flames won, though Michael and I both observed that their defense really did need some work. I knew he'd file that away for the draft. After Michael made the full rounds with the press and stopped off in the locker room, Duke invited us out to a club, but once I double checked with Daniella that she was cool to spend the night alone with Duke, Michael and I declined.

It was late. He had more shit to do in the morning, and Duke and Daniella had a couple months worth of bumping and grinding to catch up on. I wasn't sure I wanted to be the third wheel for that. They swung by the house with us so Daniella could grab her stuff. And then Michael and I were alone.

Vera had left a note saying there was food in the fridge and the puppies had been walked. They were both dead asleep, sprawled out on the living room floor, dreaming their little puppy dreams. I couldn't use them as a distraction. We needed to talk. I think we both knew it now. But I didn't know if I had a "talk" in me. I didn't even know where to start and that just made me more frustrated. This was Michael. I could tell him anything, but everything that came to mind to say felt wrong and stupid.

I held on to the counter as I toed off my shoes and then I decided on the coward's way out. "I think I'm gonna go to bed. Do you have more work to do?"

It wasn't a foolish question, but it was kinda shitty on my part. It was almost midnight on a Friday. Even Michael had his limits and we both knew it.

"No, I'm done for the day."

I glanced at him, fighting the lump forming in my chest. "Okay, well... I'm gonna head upstairs."

I didn't wait for him to respond. I just turned and tried to make for my hasty retreat but I didn't make it very far before Michael was on me. His grip on my upper arm, firm but gentle. When he turned me around all I could see was the lust storming in his eyes, but there was more.

And then I think he joined me on the Scared Shitless Express because instead of asking me for the hundredth time what was wrong or suggesting we have at least one conversation about us, he kissed me. He kissed me hard, walking me backwards toward the stairs, his hand moving along the back of my head, holding me close until my lips parted to his will. The kiss made everything worse. It made me feel reckless and trapped and so, so needy. It made me emotional.

I kinda shoved him away. Not hard, but it was definitely a push hard enough to put a little distance between us. We looked at each other, both breathing a little extra from the way his tongue had just been moving in my mouth. I didn't know what I wanted, but my body knew exactly what I needed. So I turned and ran. I made it up the stairs, but he caught me in the hallway, spinning me around again, trapping me in the cage of his arms against the wall. I looked up at him again, wanting to pull him close, wanting to push him away, but he made the decision for the both of us.

He held my gaze and he moved to his knees on the floor. He didn't tell me not to move but I could tell if I even made one step, the order would come out. He made quick work of the button and zipper on my jeans, yanking the denim down my legs. I didn't resist when he lifted my feet one by one so he could pull them off all the way. And then he was moving my underwear to the side and his mouth was on me.

I cursed, loud, grabbing on to the back of his head as he buried his face between my legs. My thighs shook but I managed to keep myself upright as he worked me over with his tongue and his lips. He pulled me closer, wrapping his arms around my body, digging the blunt tips of fingers into my ass cheeks. He was opening me up, making it harder for me to fight him, making it harder for me not to come. I gave in then and starting riding his face, shamelessly grinding against the strength of his chin. I practically sobbed when I came, calling his name, saying "Oh fuck. Jesus, fuck. Michael," as my whole body trembled.

He moved back up my body, gripping my shirt and pulling it over my head. And then he was kissing me again, letting me taste myself on his lips and his mustache as he undid my bra. He pulled away so he could tear it all the way off and then his hand gently slid up the side of my neck. I was completely naked, vulnerable and still shaking from the orgasm that wasn't entirely done with my body. His blue eyes were dark, shadowed by the dim chandelier that hung high over our heads.

"Go get on the bed." His other hand moved up from my waist and fondled my breast. My nipple was already hard, aching for his touch.

I hesitated. I was so keyed up, I wanted him right there, right then. On the marble floor or up against the wall. I didn't care. Fuck a bed.

"I don't want to hurt you on this hard floor. Go."

I turned and moved toward the bedroom, yelping when he swatted my ass. But when I turned and looked back at him, he was in anything but a playful mood. I walked backwards to the bed, scooting up the sheets, playing with myself until he was undressed enough to join me. Michael climbed on top of me. I reached down and guided him into my pussy, loving the feeling of his dick sliding through my fingers as he filled me up and stretched me.

He fucked me hard, looking me in the eye as we tested the strength of that borrowed bed, reminding me just how well we fit together. "We're gonna talk about this tomorrow," he practically growled.

"Okay," I cried out, as he hit that perfect spot just right. The intensity in his eyes forced me to look away, but I curled my legs around his waist and held him closer.

Chapter Eight

Michael was in a fucking mood when he woke up. I don't know if it was because he overslept or because Vera was the one to wake us up to tell us the driver was here. He had a day of golf and schmoozing with the Flames' GM and the mayor of Miami. We'd been up half the night screwing. I had no idea where my phone was and I doubt at any point during our sex frenzy Michael thought to pause and set his alarm.

He found both his phones in the pockets of his pants half under the bed. Sheets, and comforter edges, and trouser fabric, and our combined snoring must have muffled all the missed calls from Ruben. As he was getting dressed, cursing under his breath about how he hated golf, I threw on enough clothes to run downstairs and dig my almost dead phone out of my purse. More missed calls from numbers I didn't know, texts from Gordo asking if I was okay and texts from Kiara wanting to make sure I wasn't mad at her for the Instagram picture robbery thing.

Never. I love you to bits. I'll call you guys later, I texted her back as I walked up the stairs. I almost ran into Michael as we passed each other.

"Okay, I'm leaving," he said.

"'Kay, so I'll see you tonight?" I asked, half expecting him to say no. So much had been going on

I wouldn't be surprised if Ruben had added seven dinner meetings and a nightcap to his schedule while we were sleeping.

"Yeah, I'll try to be back in time for dinner. We still need to talk." He looked down, adjusting his belt and when he looked back up at me I could tell that oversleeping and golf weren't the only things that had gotten under his skin. I bit the inside of my lip as I nodded.

"Okay."

"I gotta go. I love you."

"Love you, too," I said to the back of his head as he disappeared down the massive stairs.

I sent Daniella a text letting her know I was up and surprisingly she was up too, and responsive.

Duke's heading to the studio early. De'Bonay is aching to record. You wanna come?

I could spend my Saturday at home with the dogs and try to get some work done. I could make myself insane by conjuring up all the different ways this eventual talk with Michael could go horribly wrong, or I could spend the day with my best friend and two international pop stars and pretend that I didn't have a care in the world. I texted Daniella back.

Yes. Send me the address. I'll have a car bring me over.

Two hours later I was pulling up to another mansion on the other side of the city. Daniella came outside to meet me. As soon as we walked inside though, it was clear that it wasn't a normal house. There was a waiting area with a concierge desk, and on the wall the words HARDROCK STUDIOS were mounted in thick dark grey lettering. I knew Duke had his own recording facilities, but I was picturing something else. The girl behind the desk smiled at us both as we slipped by.

"Isn't this place cool?" Daniella said. Duke had clearly lifted her spirits.

"It is pretty dope."

"The studio is on the lower level and then the rest is like a full service private retreat. So if the artists need a break they can hit the gym or go swim or go out back to the private beach. And there's like hotel rooms upstairs. It's really cool."

"Did you guys stay here last night?" I asked as we walked through a set of security doors. We continued down a long hallway to an elevator. It only went down. Daniella hit the button.

"No, he has this amazing suite at the Beaux Arts."

"Did you guys address the whole I love you text thing?"

"Absolutely not. He didn't bring it up so I didn't bring it up. We just fucked like rabbits. Did you guys talk?"

"Nope. Michael fucked me senseless in lieu of talking. And then he overslept and I think he was late for his tee time with the mayor, and now I think he's pissed at me." The elevator pinged and we stepped inside.

"Why? 'Cause he overslept?"

"No, 'cause he knows something's bothering me and I haven't told him yet. He's like the communication king. This whole keeping shit bottled up goes directly against his business model."

"Just talk to him. Tell him how you feel, then make up and then you can give me the green light to start planning your engagement party."

"Jesus," I groaned. "I forgot people even have those."

Daniella gave me a pity chuckle and squeezed my arm as we stepped off the elevator. "Come on."

There was another reception area, but no one was sitting there—probably since it was Saturday—and then another set of doors. We walked down to the last room and found Duke and another sound engineer sitting at the mixing board. There were two other people sitting on a massive sectional along the back wall. De'Bonay was in the booth.

I tried to keep my inner fangirl to myself as she waved at us. I'd gotten to know Duke pretty well thanks to Michael and Daniella so some of the star dust there had worn off, but De'Bonay I saw less frequently and, yeah, she was seriously the biggest chart topper in the world. With Duke behind the production I knew this album would be amazing.

They finished the take and after two more, she asked Duke if they could take a quick break. She came out of the booth and practically ran over to me. "Let me see that ring, girl!"

I offered my ring finger up before she ripped my arm out of the socket.

"It looks better in real life," she said with a

wink.

"What?" I asked.

"Oh, Jamie, let me see my phone." I remembered then that one of the women on the couch was De'Bonay's older sister. She said hi and congratulated me as she handed off her cell. De'Bonay pulled up a link to yet another gossip site. This article was pretty tame, just commenting on how Michael and I were together and recently engaged, and then they posted a few pictures from the game the night before. They'd done their best to zoom all the way in on my ring when I'd raised my hand to cover my mouth as I said something to Daniella. I'd learned from half a season of courtside games in L.A. that people loved trying to read lips.

"They really captured the thickness of my knuckles."

"Girl. Come sit, tell us everything."

"Duke, I'm sorry," I said as De'Bonay pulled me over to the couch.

"No, hey. Mike's my boy. Let's take a lunch break. You ladies talk wedding stuff." Duke winked at Daniella and then he and the sound engineer left us to our girl talk. At first, I felt a little overwhelmed, being the center of attention, but after a while I actually started to feel better. Something about talking to people who didn't know Michael that well made it easier for me to share. Jamie had her tablet and by the time Duke let us know the chef had finished preparing De'Bonay's special lunch, we were already going through different styles of wedding dresses.

We spent the rest of the afternoon listening to De'Bonay record and then when she was ready for another break, we headed out to the pool. It was so awesome watching her work. It was exactly the distraction I needed. I hadn't heard from Michael. I thought about texting him, but I knew he would text me when he was done businessing it up. That night around nine though, I cracked.

Hey Babe. We're still here at the studio. What's your dealio?

I was trying to keep it light. But he didn't respond. About thirty minutes later he just appeared in the doorway. De'Bonay had found her groove on a mid-tempo jam so I got up and went to him.

"Hey."

"Hey." We both said it to each other quietly. I didn't even have to ask. He wanted to go home. I turned and motioned to Daniella that I was gonna go. She made the universal hand gesture for "I'll text you later," and then I led Michael out to the elevator. We didn't say much on our way home. He did not enjoy golfing and he forgot to put sunscreen on the back of his neck so now he was tired, sunburnt and pissed at me. He asked if I was hungry, but I told him we'd already eaten. So had he. The mayor was eager to show off the barbeque pit he'd just put in. Once we pulled into our little beachside neighborhood, we saw Vera taking the puppies for their nightly walk.

She was right behind us when we walked in the front door. I picked up Patch as soon as he came sprinting in the door and carried him over to the couch and turned on the television. The tension between us just got worse and worse as we waited for Vera to leave. Finally she said goodnight and headed back to her room. I cut the TV off, but I couldn't bring myself to look at Michael. I chewed on my lip instead, letting Patch nibble on my fingers. The silence just stretched on.

"Kayla."

I finally looked up. Michael shrugged, his arms open wide. I hated this. He hated it too. I didn't want to talk about it, but I knew I had to.

"I feel kinda fucked up right now," I said.

"About what? Tell me. Please."

"First you can't get mad."

"I promise. I won't."

"I'm only telling you this part 'cause I'm sure it's part of the reason why I feel so strange."

"Okay."

"The twins told me you were going to propose, like way before you did."

Michael's head dropped on his shoulders and he let out a huge breath through his nose. He wasn't mad about that though. I could tell. He was just processing. He looked at the ceiling and then shook his head. "Okay, go on."

"It was an honest mistake. I was talking to them about the puppies and they said they'd already met Penny and then I dragged the rest out of them."

"Did you not want me to propose?"

"No! No." I sighed and put Patch on the floor. I had to pace. "You—you ask me for my input on everything. When we started dating we were here every step of the way." I gestured between us, eye to eye, level playing field and all. "Even with this deal you asked me first. I was just your girlfriend then. I have no say whatsoever in your business, but you asked me. But when we got here, everyone already knew. They had a freaking jersey waiting for me. *You* knew."

I knew I sounded crazy, but it was all really starting to come together in my mind, why our first week as an engaged couple felt so off.

"I knew what, baby?"

"You knew that you wanted to spend the rest of your life with me. You knew you wanted to have kids with me."

"I'm sorry. I'm trying to understand—"

"You knew weeks ago, or months ago, and you didn't tell me. You told my parents, your parents and the rest of your family and my sisters and two lawyers and Stephen and Stephen's wife and Ruben and probably Holger and PJ. You probably told Duke. You were smart to keep it from Daniella, but I'm sure you told the dogs, but you didn't tell me."

"Kayla…"

"I was sitting there in the offices of Lawn and McNamara, and it wasn't the prenup itself, but I felt so fucking uncomfortable the whole time because *you* weren't there. I'm actually glad you had it drawn up 'cause I'd box you in the street if you tried to take Patch away from me, but this is pretty much the biggest decision of both of our lives and you made it without me. We didn't talk about kids. And then after

I sign the thing we had to turn around and come here. And I'm trying to be supportive. I *hope* I'm being supportive."

"You are. You've been amazing. The last few days have been insane and you absolutely showed up."

"And I'm happy for you. This has been fun, and I can't wait to see what happens with the team next, and I even think I can learn a lot from watching you take on this new venture. But this—" I held up my hand, held up the ring. "There's been no time to even talk about this. I feel like we should have been excited about this together." I broke then, hearing the words come out of my mouth. I sounded so ridiculous. I felt selfish.

"Baby, I am excited," Michael said. "You have no idea how badly I want to be with you. Always."

I took a deep breath, trying to hold back the tears. It wasn't possible to make him understand without making it sound like I was jealous of a basketball team, which I wasn't.

"No, I do. I know you want to be with me. I know you love me. We've established that I'm funny and really fucking cute, and I'm actually a pretty dope graphic designer. The logo for the AskCupid app really needs updating by the way."

"Come here. Come sit down with me." He moved toward the kitchen stools but I shook my head.

"No. I can't."

He put up his hands in surrender. He knew. It was hard for me to talk about anything coherently when he was touching me. I knew then I had to say it, at least part of the truth, no matter how it sounded. I had to tell him how I really felt.

"God, you're just so businessy all the time. Like all the time. And it's great and it works. It works. But…Michael. That was the most unromantic proposal on the face of the Earth. And the timing, baby, it was so shit. The idea that you and I are getting married is so huge and I feel like we can't even think about it. When I try to put it out of my mind, so I can focus on you and the team, someone asks me if they can see my ring or if we've picked a date. I'm in this weird cycle of blessed and fortunate overload, but it feels more like a cycle of suck."

I think it sunk in then 'cause his expression completely dropped. Everything bubbling up inside of me, I kept to myself. The rest of what I was feeling was perilously close to insensitive and even though I wanted to kick him in the kneecap, I didn't want to say things I couldn't take back.

Michael let out a deep breath and scrubbed his hands over his face. "I'm sorry. You are absolutely right."

We both stood there for a moment, not saying anything. I didn't want to be upset with him. I didn't want to be upset period, but something felt unfinished. It occurred to me that we were finally in the middle of it, our first real fight. Like our first fight. I knew it would hurt and I knew it would suck, but I didn't know it would hurt and suck so bad. I think I took for granted just how well we got along. I couldn't wrap my mind around actually loving

Michael and being this annoyed with him or being this annoyed with anything Michael-adjacent. It felt weird. And then I just felt terrible.

"You caught me off guard in the best and the most awful way possible and since then we've barely even been alone. Daniella was asking me about engagement party stuff and I don't even know if I want one. I don't even know if *you* want one. I just wanted to talk to you about us—not like this, but about us and our future and it seems like you don't have time to do that right now. And that's fine. I'm glad you bought the team. I just wish you had actually carved out time for us. I want three kids by the way, just in case you're wondering. All girls, so tell your sperm to cooperate."

I let out another deep sigh and wiped away the tears that I'd been ignoring. Michael didn't say anything. He was still processing. Or he was thinking about a delicate way to ask for his ring back.

"Can I be this upset and still want to marry you?"

That fucking smile, just a hint of it touched his lips. "Yes. I'm pretty sure that's allowed."

"I'm sorry I didn't tell you sooner, but I didn't know how."

"I understand and I am sorry. I love you very much and I never wanted to make you feel this way."

"I'm going to get a glass of water and then I think I'm going to go to bed. I'm tired."

"Okay."

"I'm gonna hug you first though. If that's okay."

"I said come here like five minutes ago."

"Yeah, yeah." I walked into Michael's arms and let him hold me for a long time, which was a horrible idea because the emotions started swirling again and then I started fucking crying again. I still needed a little time to decompress. I let Michael kiss the top of my head and my cheeks a few times. I let him sneak one in on the lips.

"Ewww. Gross. No. Get off me," I said deadpan before I kissed him again and a few more times. "I think I'm gonna take a hot shower. Rehydrate all the ducts in my head."

I took a few steps toward the bedroom before I looked back at him. "You coming?"

"I'll be there in sec."

A sec was a little longer than I expected, but after I got out of the shower I realized how badly I needed a few moments to myself, to just breathe and process what had just happened. I think Michael needed it too. I was bone tired by the time I climbed between our sheets, but I couldn't fall asleep until Michael climbed in the bed with me. He came to upstairs eventually, brought the puppies with him, one under each arm. Then we turned on Jurassic Park. I let him hold me while we watched it together, but soon, I fell asleep.

In the middle of the night all my hydrating hit me. I

woke up to run to the restroom, but stopped when I realized Michael was sitting on the edge of the bed. Penny was dead asleep but he was gently petting her side.

"Babe?" I whispered.

"Yes, baby."

"You okay?"

When he didn't answer I crawled across the sheets and sat beside him on the bed.

"What's up?"

He shook his head. "Just having some revelations."

"About?"

"You and me." He leaned over and laid a long lingering kiss on my forehead. "I never thought I'd meet you."

"Yeah same, but I'm glad we did. Even if it took me being ridiculously broke."

He went on, but kept his eyes trained on the floor. "I'm sorry I didn't make this special for you. When I was a kid, when something scared me my dad would tell me to break it down into pieces. He'd tell me to take care of the pieces I could handle on my own and then if I had pieces left over I should ask for help. I got so good at taking care of the big pieces on my own, after so many years, I've grown accustomed to not asking for help, even when I'm terrified."

"Does marriage scare you that bad?" I swallowed nervously. Maybe my little freak out had been more than he wanted to deal with for the next fifty years.

"No, but losing you does. When Sands called

about buying the team all I could think about was you and I had this crystal clear moment: marry Kayla, have kids with her, fuck up Holger's whole job description. And then immediately all I could think of was you saying no."

"Babe."

"And then when I convinced myself that that wasn't likely considering all the poetry you've written about my genitals, all I could think about was screwing this up. I had this... vision of me becoming this man that I'm not. Unfaithful, inattentive, and then I reminded myself that would never happen considering all the poetry I've secretly written about your amazing tits and that butt that just won't quit. They're saved on my phone, but I haven't gotten up the nerve to send them to you yet. They're not as good as yours."

"You'll have to show me someday. I'm sure they're great."

"They'll take the place of my vows. But yeah, I thought about just not being enough." He turned to me and I could barely breathe. His voice was steady, but there were tears in his eyes threatening to spill over. "I look at you and you—you are pure sunshine, Kayla Renee Davis. I think about how happy you make me and I'm terrified that I'm not enough. I was so scared you'd leave me before we never really got started. So. I took that fear and broke it apart into pieces. Talked to your parents first so they wouldn't hate me even more. And then I bought a ring and then the prenup and then we went to Half Moon Bay so I could catch my breath. The alternative was frisbee throwing the prenup at you and hiding behind Holger while you looked it over."

"You wouldn't do that." I laughed quietly.

"I strongly considered it. My love for you isn't something to be scared of, though. I'm just an old man who didn't think to fight against his old habits."

"You know, I love you just as much. It scares me too. I went from not even really thinking about dating to stumbling upon this amazing man who luckily turned out to be absolutely perfect for me. You're my butter pecan apple pie a la mode. You're so sweet. I love you so much. And my parents don't hate you."

"Your father doesn't, but your mom is firmly on the fence."

"You'll wear her down. I'm sure of it."

I leaned up and kissed him, then wiped away his tears. And then he wiped away mine. We were a mess, the two of us.

"You know what I realized? I actually hate surprises. Even surprises I kinda know about. How about we don't surprise each other anymore? Let's be one of those couples that everyone hates. One of those couples that are so transparent with each other it's kinda creepy. Like we tell each other stuff, like when we're scared or when we're unsure. I'll tell you ninety weeks in advance about my plan to eventually get a cat and you can mention that maybe you want to spend our first anniversary somewhere with snow."

"Do you want that?"

"Sweet god, yes. Why is it so fucking hot down

here?"

"Can't be helped, I'm afraid."

"We're a team, yeah? I have the ill-fitting jerseys to prove it."

"We are. I can't promise I'll never surprise you again. I wouldn't feel right going a lifetime without catching my lady a little off guard every now and then. But no more taking things apart without you."

"I love the sound of that. Now. I need to know. Do you need help getting back to sleep?"

"Do you have something particular in mind?"

"Fucking. We should fuck until we're sleepy again. But first. I have to pee." I jumped up and ran to the bathroom, the deep sound of Michael's quiet laughter finally making me feel whole again.

I moved a little closer to Michael on the stone bench. "Comfortable?" he asked.

"Actually my ass is killing me, thank you very much."

"You were the one begging for it last night. If I remember clearly you said something along the lines of fuck me harder. And then you added a please."

"Yeah, whatever."

Michael laughed, then pulled me a little closer. "Smile," he whispered.

He'd been completely right. By the following Monday morning the media had completely forgotten about us. Nothing exciting had happened, but the twenty-four hour click bait cycle made us old news after forty-eight hours. The fact that neither Michael nor I responded to the crappy comments about our interracial relationship only hastened the process. People were dicks, but we weren't going to waste our time schooling racists on the Internet when we had our own lives to enjoy.

We talked and talked some more, and spent as much time together as possible. We both still had work upon work to do, but we were able to figure out some important things. No engagement party, but that didn't stop us from getting a ton of gifts from celebs and athletes and random tech CEOs. We were going to do a small wedding, just friends and family, and we were going to do it in Michigan. Doing it there, close to his family, just felt right. And we talked about kids. Three, we both agreed. We'd get started as soon as we got K&D off the ground for real and hired a few more employees to help Daniella out with operations and me with design.

After I finished the whole line for Queer Qards, I suggested a trip to visit Michael's parents. We could scout wedding locations while we were there, and during our flight up North, I admitted to Michael there *was* one thing I wanted: engagement photos. His parents' backyard on the lake provided the perfect setting.

"Kayla if you can, just move your hand a little to the right. Penny?" Our photographer, Shannon asked.

"That's Patch."

"Yes, sorry, the adorable Patch's head is blocking your ring." I slid my hand a little further up Michael's forearm.

"Is that better?"

"Perfect." It had been over a month since we picked them up at the shelter and they were still hyper as puppies can be, but both Penny and Patch had mastered simple commands. They were behaving so well for our little family photo shoot.

We went for another hour, moving around the yard and the edge of the lake, before Michael and I were satisfied with the variety of shots she'd taken. We saw Shannon off and then headed back inside to join Michael's family for dinner. I squirmed as Michael's hand moved over my ass.

"Behave yourself," I grumbled as we slipped through the back door.

"With you?" He leaned down and nipped my neck. "Never."

The End

What's Next from Rebekah

Check out Kayla and Michael's final chapter, SO FOR REAL!

Chapter One

I learned a lot about myself while I was planning our wedding. I learned a whole lot about my family. Like how my little sisters, Kaleigh and Kiara, were willing to actually murder each other for the title of Maid of Honor. I also learned that my mother was completely prepared to disown me if I thought for one second that my fiancé, Michael, and I were going to exchange vows anywhere other than an actual church.

I learned that marrying an actual billionaire came with some interesting perks and requests, like having your engagement photos in the Times and your wedding photos exclusively featured in the most popular women's magazine in the country.

I learned that when you had a best friend like Daniella, she was the right choice for Maid of Honor because she actually made the best go-between with my overzealous aunts and my butt hurt roommates from college, who I literally hadn't spoken to in five years, but invited anyway. I learned that Daniella was really awesome at making lists and delegating tasks and deflecting nonsense, and I had to keep her as my best friend forever and buy her an expensive exotic animal or a boat. Michael and I would have eloped without her.

There was an amazing engagement party. Two actually—marrying rich was weird. A fun as hell bachelorette party and the best bridal shower a girl could ask for. So many details I'd never considered, but when the day came, I could only think of one thing: I was marrying Michael Bradbury. The way we met, at a Sugar baby/Sugar Daddy cocktail party two summers before, both awkward and uncomfortable and completely out of our elements. What we both wanted and how we each ended up being exactly what the other needed. I never could have imagined it this way. Never in a million years.

Our engagement had lasted a little over a year. My mother had a guest list to review and opinions on flowers and accessories, and this was her first baby walking down the aisle. She would not be rushed. In that year, I became more and more secure in the fact that Michael was the perfect man for me. His ridiculously good looks aside, even when I tried looking, there was no flaw to be found, or maybe our flaws just meshed so perfectly.

Michael opened up more, letting his guard down, letting me be my true self. I don't know when it happened or how, but suddenly he was my person, the one I could tell anything and everything, the one I consulted first, and even though he tried to spare me the details of his business deals, he started to really turn to me when he was undecided or just needed to vent. He knew he could tell me when his mother's deteriorating health was eating him up inside, how sometimes he felt like the shittiest brother and the shittiest absentee uncle because sometimes he could only send gifts and money when his job made a pitstop to the midwest impossible.

We built a trust, something I'd never experienced with anyone else before. He was mine and I was his, lover and best friend, my soulmate, the filling in my heart pie, and we got to kick it together until death do us part. I couldn't wait to spend the rest of our lives together. I was fucking excited just to start.

Our wedding week was a blur. Once we arrived in Michigan, it felt like a race to some sort of bizarre finish line and luckily we made it, incident free. Everyone showed up, everyone looked great. No special vows, just the word the church had to offer, by the book, but I was feeling a tad sentimental so I tasked my cousin, Julianne, with noting the exact time the Reverend pronounced us husband and wife. It was five thirty-four p.m. I told her to write it down and email it to me, too. I didn't want there to be any chance that I would forget.

It took everyone a little while to make their way out of the church. We waited with our wedding party as our photographer, Shannon, got us situated on the elaborate steps that wrapped around St. Andrew's Episcopal. She had a plan that involved a particular set of birch-encased windows. I grabbed Michael's hand and held it to the side of my neck. I'd been a mix of happy and nervous for the last few months, but nothing prepared me for just how excited I'd be once I became a Mrs.

"Can you feel that?"

I knew he could. My pulse was actually pounding.

"I can." He kissed me again quickly on the lips, then smiled. "Don't pass out on me, okay?"

"I promise I won't. Are you okay?"

I couldn't stop looking at him. Everything else around us was moving in high speed, but all I could see was him. Michael was standing there in front of me on the church's brick steps in stark high def, slow motion. His color was way up and his eyes were still a little watery. I knew he was going through his own range of emotions, but he was my husband now. Checking on his general welfare was my duty.

"You look like you sniffed some real good shit," I teased, then kissed him again.

"I don't think I can explain how more than okay I am right now. I love you."

"I love you." I leaned up on my toes and kissed him some more. When he pulled away just a little, I realized our whole wedding party was perfectly positioned around us and Shannon had already started snapping away. We took a million more pictures while Zia, my new friend and traveling makeup artist, and Malika, our wedding planner, directed our guests over to the Paultin Conservatory for the reception.

Laughing at the jokes Michael's friend Duke and Daniella's sister Lili would not stop cracking during our photo session helped calm my nerves and level me out a bit, but I was still plenty flustered when Michael and I finally climbed into our private car. Finally, it was just the two of us. I turned to my husband, but before I could get a word out he pulled me into his lap and started hiking up the miles and miles of flowy fabric I was wearing.

I had picked the dress for comfort and ease over style, but the lace and chiffon were still gorgeous. A little revealing up top, with a plunging neckline. I figured we'd be so busy with smiling and thanking people and making small talk that Michael wouldn't even get the opportunity to look under the hood until we got to our honeymoon suite much, much later that night. Holy shit, was I wrong.

"What are you doing?" His lips on my neck made it a little hard to breathe again.

His hand slipped roughly up my thigh. I spread my legs and arched toward his searching fingers, even though I knew we shouldn't. The Conservatory wasn't that far away.

"You're not wearing that spanx thing, are you?" Before I could even answer, his hand was groping my crotch. He already had his answer. Again, the day was about comfort. Full body, inch thick, tighter-than-skin spandex spelled anything but comfort to me. I'd opted for a pair of lace panties that offered a hint of sexiness while providing the butt coverage needed to keep the fabric from riding clean up my ass while I tried to out Cha Cha Slide my sisters during the reception.

Michael pulled the lace aside and gently fondled my suddenly swollen lips. It only took a few strokes before I was soaking wet. He slid a finger inside me and then pulled it out again, once and then again before his fingers moved over my clit.

"No. Oh god, babe. We have to get over to the reception," I said. The car was still idling at the curb.

"No, the fuck we don't. Not yet."

"But we have to do the...the whole grand entrance." I bit down on my smudge proof lip tint to smother a desperate moan. His erection was pressing against my ass, through the fabric of his suit. We were still technically in the middle of our wedding and we had people waiting for us.

"Michael—" He silenced me with another deep kiss before he pulled back and looked me in the eye.

"Kayla. Baby. Relax. I talked to Zia. I talked to Daniella who is gonna talk to Malika. I talked to my sister. I talked to the driver. I just want one minute with my wife. There is booze and entertainment. There is plenty to keep everyone busy. Please—" I gasped as two fingers pushed deep inside of my pussy. "Let me enjoy the first few minutes of married life with my wife."

Okay, what he was saying was nice, but the way he smiled, so smug, so satisfied, so happy when he said the words "my wife," all while stroking me in the most dirty of ways...I almost came on his hand right then.

"Well," I groaned as I wrapped my arm around his shoulder to help steady myself on his lap. "I think you're right. I'm sorry. I'm still in responsible bride mode. I want more than a few minutes alone with you, too." I'd been so focused on blowing his mind during our honeymoon, I'd put the option of quality pants-off time out of my mind until then. But part of me had forgotten who I was dealing with. This was

Michael Bradbury, and with him, as long as you didn't violate any law of public indecency, any time was pants-off time. I shifted closer, spreading my legs even wider until my knees were hooked on either side of his thighs.

"Have I mentioned that I love you?"

"I—" I couldn't speak. Michael had my clit gently between his fingers. I was going to come any second. My hip swirled against his hand, my aching muscles desperate for more. A strong orgasm tackled my senses, forcing me to press my forehead against Michael's as I shuddered through the pleasure. "I love you too," I whimpered.

Michael's lips found mine again, his kisses probably the best and worst thing to help me come down. His cock was still hard against my leg when I could finally see straight. I kept on kissing him, but slid off his lap and went right for his belt. I was so glad he'd decided on a simple suit and not a tux with a ton of unnecessary pieces like a cummberbund or a vest. His erection practically popped into my hand as he wiggled his pants and boxer briefs out of the way. His dick was hard and thick, enough to fill one hand and long enough to stroke with two. I gripped him firm, feeling him up and down as I watched the satisfied look on his face.

"Don't fuck up my hair," I instructed him with a deadly glare before I leaned over his lap. "I mean it."

"I won't, baby." His laugh turned into a groan. Zia finished my makeup off with some type of outdoor deck sealant so my wedding day face isn't going anywhere, blow job or no, but my hair was another matter. It would have been obvious if Michael had gotten a desperate handful. As I traced the head of his cock a few times with my tongue, he followed my strict orders, toying with the row of pearl buttons running down the deceptively sheer fabrics covering my back.

I rushed. I knew I did. No matter what he told who, my mom raised a good southern girl and at the very least she would say it was rude to keep that many people waiting too long. Especially when Michael and I had ten days of no-pants time and butt stuff just around the corner. I sucked him deep and hard, and stroked him the desperate way he liked when we both got a little rough and carried away. I did the one thing I knew would drive him crazy—I looked him in the eye while I was jerking him. I saw the tension spread across his forehead and his fingers spread wide on my back. He knew better than to pop one of my buttons. He refused to close his eyes when he came. They narrowed to small slits as he cursed and groaned my name, filling my mouth with every drop he had.

He had clearly thought of everything 'cause there was a festively decorated basket in one of the jump seats. I didn't notice it at first, but Michael handed me some water and mints, then cleaned himself up with some wet wipes. There was lotion, something I'd made a serious part of his life, and when we were all fresh and tidy—my hair still perfectly in place—Michael cracked the door and told the driver we were ready to go.

He settled back in the seat next to me and took my hand, brushing his lips against my knuckles before he kissed the back of my hand. I was still a little high from my orgasm but those small, sweet gestures made me want to cry all the tears that hadn't escaped during our simple vows.

"Is this what married life is going to be like with you, Mr. Bradbury?" I teased.

"Mrs. Bradbury," he said before he kissed me on the temple. "This life will be whatever you want it to be. Just tell me and it's yours."

The billions lining his bank account made that statement absolutely doable, but I believed him because I knew he loved me just that much.

Yeah, yeah saying our vows was great and shit, but I think Michael and I had the best reception in the history of wedding receptions. The food was delicious and plentiful, a fancy spin on southern barbecue with gluten free and vegetarian options. DJ Makeway took a break from his world tour to spin and emcee. Michael and I shared our first dance to a new favorite off De'bonay's most recent album. Of course she was there to sing it for us live. Kiara and Kaleigh, and Myra and Matthew made the most adorable toasts and I couldn't help but weep like a baby because my heart was full to bursting. I knew how lucky Michael and I were. We both had great families and now the number of sweet, caring people in our lives had officially doubled.

I danced with my dad to some mix he'd rigged up with the DJ, a combo of Stevie Wonder's "Isn't She Lovely" and Prince's "1999," both bathtime favorites when I was a kid. Michael's mom Nina still struggled in her ongoing battle with dementia, but she was in great spirits and let Michael twirl her around the dance floor to a James Taylor classic. After that I made a pact with Michael because we've been to enough social functions together. No separating. We worked the room together, hand in hand greeting our families and friends. Team Bradbury FTW. We skipped cutting a cake because it was such a weird tradition to me and Michael wasn't too hung up on it either and instead treated our guests to a sweets bar with all the mini cupcakes and brownies and tarts they could handle.

I fought against it at first, but Michael's business partner and his wife, insisted on arranging a gifting suite for our guests. I mean there are goodie bags and then there are bags with nearly fifteen thousand dollars worth of free shit, but when my fifteen-year-old cousin came running up to me, losing his shit because he never thought he'd have a smartwatch, I remembered again that having money was not a bad thing. As the night stretched on, Michael and I made a stealth exit. We had plans for brunch with our families and whichever guests decided to hang around the following morning, but finally it was *US* time.

We'd already been in Michigan for a little over a week, staying at a large rental with Holger, our primary housekeeper, and our dogs Patch and Penny, but that night we checked into this adorable honeymoon suite at a local hotel Michael's sister had picked out for us. Daniella and my mom told me a hundred times that they would take care of everything and Ruben, Michael's personal assistant, teamed with Holger to make sure all of our clothes and personal odds and ends were there waiting for us. There were other surprises waiting when we opened the honeymoon suite door.

Michael stepped behind me and immediately started unbuttoning my dress. I shivered as his lips traced over my bare shoulder. I was exhausted and champagne drunk, but this was a moment I'd been waiting for for over a year. Making love to my husband.

"I have strict instructions," he whispered against my skin as he gently gripped the fabric that had pooled around my waist and pushed it down to the floor.

"From who?" I covered my boobs, doing my best to spare Michael from the boob lift tape pads we had to rig up so I could wear my dress without a bra.

"Daniella."

"And what were her instructions?"

"To treat you like the most precious thing in my world."

"Is that so?"

"It is. If you'll follow me." Michael took my hand, laughing a bit as I was forced to reveal the horrible price my tits had paid for fashion. We walked through the main sitting room, into the bedroom and then further into the massive bathroom. I glanced back at the bedroom. There were candles lit and rose petals everywhere. It looked so nice.

"Where are we going?" I asked impatiently. "The bed is right here. Let's have sex on the bed."

"And we will, I promise." Michael smiled that half smile this time. He was humoring me. I turned back and saw what he was getting at. Lit candles and rose petals in the bathroom too. There were two plush bath robes hanging on a hook outside the huge walk-in shower and all sorts of toiletries arranged on the vanity counters. Michael gently helped me pull the breast form thingies off my boobs and then he pulled my underwear down. I stepped out of them and walked into the big fluffy towel Michael was holding open for me. I secured it around my chest and looked up at him.

"We're halfway there. Now you just take off your pants at least and we can make this man and wife shit real official."

"On the counter, please, if you will."

I shook my head at him, but shuffled up on the sturdy marble surface. Michael made a show of slowly removing his suit jacket and then his tie.

"We're gonna see if I'm any good at this."

"At what??" I laughed.

He ignored me and grabbed a little folded card hidden among the toiletries, then started searching like he was about to bake a cake. When he turned back to me, he was holding a small cloth and a really expensive bottle of makeup remover.

"If you'll close your eyes please. We can begin."

I did what he asked but I still laughed at him a little. "Babe, this is the weirdest foreplay. I could have taken off my own makeup."

"I was talking to Daniella and Zia about how much I love you and Zia mentioned that if I really loved you, I'd make sure that you didn't fall asleep with all this stuff on." I nodded as he went on. I usually liked to scrub off a layer of my face when I was getting ready for bed at night, but he was being so gentle. "I thought about our usual nightly rituals and the pact we'd made and how for the next two weeks I have no reason to leave your side."

My eyes popped open and I looked up at him. I thought my chest was going to cave in.

"I knew I would either forget or get caught up in trying to dick you down something special because it's our wedding night, damn right I have something to prove and then you'd wake up, and—"

"I'd roll out of bed groaning and complaining about how gross my face feels and you'd feel extra guilty for not reminding me?"

"Exactly. When we get back—"

"Don't say it," I said throwing my head back dramatically, which was a big mistake because I was still pretty tipsy.

"Okay, I won't. But we both know."

"So you help me take off my makeup and tomorrow I help you shave and we're one of those married couples who make people want to barf."

"We're a husband and wife who actually love each other. I married you because I want to be with you. Always. But since *always* isn't exactly possible, I'll have to settle for as often as possible."

I was too choked up to say anything sweet or even witty back so I just nodded and closed my eyes again, letting a few fat tears of joy run down my face as he finished the job.

And then he took the forty-eight pins out of my half updo and let me undress him. We showered together, kissing and caressing, teasing each other until we couldn't take it anymore.

He was hard, erection standing at attention as he led me back into the bedroom. More champagne, a private toast to our future, to us. There was something really hot about watching my husband partake in the bubbly while standing in front of me, butt naked. I told him as much and that seemed to be the end of his patience. Michael and I finally made love. We'd had sex the day before, but this time it was married sex and it was freaking amazing.

After, he dug up my silk scarf and lay beside me stroking my side and thigh as I preserved the super expensive eighteen inch bundles I'd bought just for the occasion. When he finally cut off the lights it was technically a new day, but I still wanted to include those couple of hours past midnight, those precious minutes, as part of the best day of my life.

About the Author

Rebekah was raised in Southern New Hampshire and now lives in Southern California with a great human, one cat whom she loves dearly and another cat she wants to take back to the shelter.

Her interests include Wonder Woman collectibles, cookies, James Taylor, whatever Nicki Minaj is doing at any given moment, quality hip-hop, football, American muscle cars, large breed dogs, and the ocean. When she's not working, writing, reading, or sleeping, she is watching HGTV and cartoons, or taking dance classes. If given the chance, she will cheat at UNO.

You can find more stories by Rebekah at rebekahweatherspoon.com